CHAS WILLIAMSON

Seeking Series: Book Three

SEEKING
Eternity

Copyright © 2018 Chas Williamson
All Rights Reserved

Print ISBN: 978-1-949150-08-7
eBook ISBN: 978-1-949150-09-4

Year of the Book
135 Glen Avenue
Glen Rock, PA 17327

This is a work of fiction. Names, characters, businesses, places, events and incidents are either the products of the author's imagination or used in a fictitious manner. Any resemblance to actual persons, living or dead, or actual events is purely coincidental.

Dedication

This book is dedicated to my love, the girl I fell for long before I knew your name, my true soulmate. I have been so blessed to find you when we were young, to fall head over heels in love with you, to live through the trials, joys and adventures of life with you at my side. If I were to wake up and find this all a dream and it is a bright September day in 1976 once more, know I would do it all over again, in less than a heartbeat. You are my dream come true, my best friend, my partner, my world. Not just in this life, but for all eternity.

> *When the grasses have all withered,*
> *after the stars have all burned out,*
> *when the universe is just a dim memory,*
> *know I will still be in love with you,*
> *forever and ever,*
> *even after eternity passes away.*

Acknowledgments

To God, for blessing me with the dream, the connections, the faith and surrounding me with the right people at the right time. Truly, You have a master plan, which You see through in Your time.

To my wife and best friend. Thank you for encouraging my dreams and making them come true.

To my son, the conqueror of all things technical.

To my daughter, the expert in the field of medicine.

To those who encouraged and believed in me.

To my beta readers, Connie, Mary, Sarah and Janet, for your guidance and advice.

To Demi, my publisher, editor and friend. Thank you for all your help and guidance.

To J.R.R. Tolkien, Tom Clancy, Debbie Macomber, Aldous Huxley and hundreds of other authors, whose stories I devoured, enchanting me with tales of adventure, far-off lands and magical places. Your inspiring stories encouraged the love of writing in my heart. I am honored to be an author because of you.

Chapter 1

Stanley Jenkins collapsed into his recliner. It was Thanksgiving and he had so much to be thankful for. The others were clearing off the table in the next room. One voice stood out above all the others. *Nora.* He could hear his wife's melodious laugh as she talked and played with their children and grandchildren. His entire family... four daughters, their husbands, and all nineteen grandchildren were in the house. He was full, not only in his stomach, but in his heart.

Stan clicked the remote, turning on the television to watch the Detroit Lions host the Minnesota Vikings, but his mind really wasn't on football. It kept drifting back to reflect on his wonderful life and many blessings.

The greatest of those blessings was Nora. He'd fallen in love the first day he caught a glimpse of her in high school, now so many years ago. Stan had lost her once and almost a second time, but now she was his lifelong mate.

The game was playing on TV, but his mind wandered through his vast collection of memories.

A soft, happy voice derailed his train of thought. "Hey Daddy, how're you doing? Brought you a cup of coffee with the pumpkin spice creamer you love so much. Get enough to eat?" It was Kaitlin, his youngest. She kissed his forehead and sat next to him.

He reached for her hand. His baby, now grown and a mother of her own. "Katie, I ate way too much! Might need to open the top of my pants so I can be comfortable."

Kaitlin laughed, her whole face beaming. *So good to see her smile.* For too many years she had been lonely and unhappy. Then Jeremy came into her life. She seemed to be in heaven now. Kaitlin repositioned herself on the seat, obviously trying to find a comfortable position.

Stan gently patted his daughter's hand. "How's my newest grandbaby doing today?"

Her smile increased in width. "Oh, this one's gonna be a boy. By the feel of it, he'll be a soccer star or a placekicker." They talked for a little while longer until one of her twins started to cry in the next room. She squeezed his hand. "Be right back, Daddy. Gotta go figure out who did what to whom." Kaitlin giggled and gave his forehead another kiss.

Stan tried to concentrate on the game, but he was suffering from a bad case of heartburn. *Too much turkey.* His left arm was painful. The headache he'd woken up with in the morning was getting worse, and now his jaw hurt a little bit, too.

The Lions drove the ball deep into Minnesota's red zone. It was first and goal from the two. The center snapped the ball. The quarterback dropped into the pocket, looking for an open receiver. He lofted a soft pass to the near side of the end zone, but the Minnesota safety picked off the pass, running it all the way back, untouched, for a touchdown. Stan cursed under his breath.

Suddenly, sharp pain exploded in his chest. It rippled down his left arm as if caught in a wringer. Everything became blurry. Stan released his coffee mug so he could grasp his arm. The sudden urge to throw up was accompanied by the new wave of pain that rolled over him.

The room started to spin. Nora's beautiful face suddenly appeared before him. He leaned forward to touch her but the pain convulsed his arms. *This is it. I love you, Nora!* The world turned black before everything disappeared.

Chapter 2

*S*tan walked into school that September morning to the smell of old books and cut grass. This was it, his first day at Eastern Detroit High School. Earlier that summer, Stan's parents had moved into an old, tiny house on a crowded street. The new high school was gigantic. Stan had never seen so many kids before in his life.

Stan jumped out of the way to avoid two teenagers chasing each other with wild abandon. There was a time when that would have been him, with the gang he used to run around with. *That was before...* Thank goodness for Jeff, his new best friend. Jeff lived two doors down. It hadn't taken long for them to become fast friends. At least he had someone to hang around.

Stan and Jeff arrived early so they could walk around the school halls, checking out the girls. My, but this school had some beautiful chicks! He and Jeff were compiling a list of which ones they thought were the cutest. It was almost time to head to their homerooms when Stan spotted her. It was as if time stood still.

Her brown hair was cut short. Her expressive eyes were hazel. She was walking and talking with a couple of other girls, but this one... well she was absolutely gorgeous in Stan's mind!

But it wasn't how she looked that caught his attention. It seemed as if there was a spotlight shining down on her from Heaven. She laughed at some joke or comment and when she did, her face lit up.

She didn't seem to notice him, but Stan stopped. His heart fluttered as he watched her walk by. Jeff had continued to walk and talk, but Stan was glued to the floor like a statue. His eyes and then his whole body turned to watch the girl walk away.

Jeff suddenly realized Stan wasn't by his side. "Whatcha doing, Stan the man?"

He had to struggle to breathe as he pointed at the brunette. "That girl. You know who she is?"

"Of course," Jeff nodded. "That's Nora Thomas. Everyone knows her. What's up?"

Stan smiled as he watched her walk away. He slowly said, as if savoring her name, "Nora Thomas. Jeff, I swear to you, I'm gonna marry that girl some day!"

Jeff shook his head. "Uh, might want to re-think that one."

Stan was still watching as she receded from view. When she turned a corner, Stan turned to face Jeff. "Why would I want to re-think anything? Did you see how beautiful she is?"

Jeff nodded, but frowned. "Yeah, Nora is a beautiful chick, but leave her alone."

"Why?" Stan questioned.

"Do you know who Nebraska's All-American middle linebacker is?"

"Yeah, everybody's heard of him. He graduated from here, something Crittenbill."

"Crittendale. Robert Crittendale."

"Yeah, I knew it was something like that. Why do you ask?"

"He's Nora's fiancé."

Chapter 3

*H*aving resolved the twins' latest crisis, Kaitlin waddled back into the room to watch the game with her father. She was puzzled as she saw him reach toward the TV. Her puzzlement turned to fear when the coffee cup fell from his hand. Her father crumpled back into the easy chair.

She grabbed his arm and shook it. "Daddy, you okay? Daddy?" No response. This wasn't good. Kaitlin screamed for her sister. She was a nurse. "Kelly, get in here! Help! Help!"

Her screams brought most of the adults. Her husband Jeremy was there first, followed closely by the second youngest sister. Kelly immediately assessed the situation, feeling for vital signs.

Kaitlin could see the change occur in her sister's face as Kelly screamed, "Quick! Cassie, call 911! Daddy's having a heart attack! He's not breathing. No pulse! Get him out of the chair and flat on the floor!"

Jeremy and Kelly's husband, Geeter, lifted him out of the recliner, gently placing him on the carpet. Kelly kneeled next to Stan and began chest compressions.

***

Even though Jeff told him she was engaged, Stan was totally enamored with Nora. He kept a constant watch out for her in the halls, but as the months slipped by, he hadn't caught another glimpse of her.

Borrowing Jeff's yearbook from the previous year, he scoured the pages for her picture. It took him a while to find her because in her junior class picture, her hair was really long. Stan found she was wearing dark glasses. She was also standing partially behind some other kids.

When he'd seen her that first morning, her hair was much shorter and she wasn't wearing glasses. It didn't matter how long her hair was or if she had glasses, she was beautiful.

He found out Nora was active in the Future Librarians Club as well as the debate team. He searched every page in the yearbook for more photos, but those three were the only ones he could find. He dreamed about meeting her and hoped when he did, she would immediately feel the same way.

Stan asked Jeff to help him find out more about her, but Jeff refused. "Ever meet Bob Crittendale?" Stan shook his head no. "The guy is like six foot five and weighs about two hundred and fifty pounds. He was second team All-American in his junior year! That girl is off limits, Stan, off limits. You do get that, don't you?"

Stan nodded, but his heart whispered, *"We'll see about that."*

Fate seemed to give Stan a break when the second semester ended. His fourth period English class changed from Mark Twain to Science-Fiction studies. Stan switched to a different lunch period for both Mondays and Thursdays. On the second Monday of January, as he left the restroom at lunch, he saw her. She was talking to a bunch of her friends in the lobby.

Stan's mouth turned dry. Now what? *I've got to talk to her.* He wracked his mind to figure out how to get her attention. He looked around and recognized one of the girls Nora was speaking with, Judy Allison. Judy was a senior in his Sci-Fi class. This was his 'in'! Stan decided he would 'accidentally' meet Nora. He had butterflies in his stomach when he walked over to the girls.

It took a few minutes before Judy noticed him. "Hi, Stan! What do you think of the class?"

Now that he was this close to Nora, he began to get cold feet. He spoke to Judy, but his eyes couldn't leave the brunette's face. "Sure, Judy, I, uh, I find it interesting." Nora was even prettier than he remembered!

Judy suddenly laughed at him, asking, "Stan, you think it's cold in here?"

Actually, Stan's face was flushed because he was a little embarrassed. He wished he had thought through what he wanted to say a little bit more. "Uh, no. Why? Are you cold?"

The other girls were all starting to snicker, except Nora, who gave him a genuine smile. "I'm not the least bit cold," Judy said, "but I think you might be a little chilly, you know, down there!" She pointed to his crotch.

Stan looked and saw his zipper was down!

"Oh my God," he squealed. He turned his back and pulled up his zipper. His face was bright red as he slunk away in embarrassment.

Then the most beautiful voice he had ever heard said, "Stan, don't leave. And don't pay any attention to my friends. It's not like they never did something stupid, you know?"

Stan turned, finding Nora right behind him. She'd followed him! His mouth dropped open. Nora Thomas was talking to him!

She stuck out her hand and smiled, "Hi, I'm Nora Thomas. It's such a pleasure to meet you."

Her smile lit up his world. She was so pretty that he couldn't answer.

"It's okay," she laughed. "Are you new here? I don't think we've met before." Her hand was still extended to him.

Stan's face turned so hot he thought he might pass out. He finally came to his senses. He took her hand and shook it, too hard. "It is really good to finally meet you, Nora. My name is Stanley Jenkins, but you can call me Stanley Jenkins. Darn it! I mean, please call me Stan." Inside, he chided himself. *I must look like a fool to her.*

Nora laughed before smiling widely. "Finally meet me? What do you mean, Stan?"

"I mean, I, uh, I have seen you around a couple of times. Well, only once, really."

Her smile didn't leave her face, but she looked puzzled.

How could any girl be this beautiful? She had to be an angel.

"You saw me one time? When?"

"Uh, the first day of school."

"And you remembered me?" Her face slowly turned pink. "Did I make a lasting impression on you?"

He nodded.

The pink slowly turned a deep red. "Was it a good or bad impression?"

"Good, very good." They talked for the next five minutes before his lunch bell rang. Afterwards, Stan couldn't recall anything about the conversation. But he could remember her eyes, her pretty face and the way she smiled at him.

***

After a warm farewell, they headed back to their respective classes. Judy said to her, "I think Stanley likes you, Nora!"

Nora felt her cheeks heat. "Well, he's very nice, you know?"

Her friend gave her a knowing look. "No, silly! I don't mean like that. I meant he really, really *likes* you!"

Really? Nora's heart skipped a beat. She tried to calm herself, replying, "Oh Judy, why can't girls and boys just be friends?" But a warmth spread across her chest as she thought about him.

***

Stan couldn't stop thinking about Nora after that first day. In fact, he couldn't think about anything else. The following Thursday, Stan was suffering from a major case of nervousness. Stan carried his tray and looked for a place to sit. As he surveyed the cafeteria, he realized someone was waving at him. *Nora.* Sitting all alone at a table, she motioned for him to come sit with her. Again, his face blushed, but he sat with her.

"Stan, it's great to see you! Judy told me you're in her Science-Fiction class. Is this your new lunch time?"

Stan opened his mouth, but nothing came out. He could only nod.

"Great! We could plan on having lunch together every Monday and Thursday. Would that be all right?"

Again, Stan could only nod.

Nora studied him. A puzzled smile slowly covered her face. "Do you have laryngitis or something? I mean, you can talk, can't you?" Her smile grew and she laughed her beautiful laugh.

He opened his mouth to speak, but nothing came out. Stan nodded once again.

By this time, some of her friends sat with them. The chatter around the table was about the school's basketball team, which was currently undefeated.

Stan's voice finally returned. "Nice weather lately, huh?" *Nice weather? I'm a stupid idiot.*

Nora's eyes sparkled. She gave him her full attention instead of talking with the other girls.

Lunch passed quickly, much too quickly for Stan. He had been looking forward to the weekend, but suddenly wished it were Monday.

Over the next few weeks, they became very, very close friends. Stan had never shared as much or talked as meaningfully as he did with her. Even about the tough stuff.

"Did you go on vacation last summer?" she asked.

He blushed. "No, my parents haven't ever taken me on vacation."

"I'm sorry. If I could, I would take you on a vacation. They're so much fun."

He studied the floor. "My parents struggle to make ends meet. That was why they sold our home. It was really big. Now we rent a small rancher."

Her hand touched his chin. "I'm sorry things are tough on your parents. But I don't care if they're rich or poor. I like you."

Stan watched her face in disbelief. "I... I don't know what to say."

Nora laughed. "Don't say anything."

"Okay. You talk. Did you go on vacation last year?"

Nora told him about their family trip to California. The following lunch period, she brought in a photo album from her vacation. Photography was one of her hobbies and Stan could tell she was very talented with a camera.

As he paged through her album, her hand brushed against his. In a moment of stupidity, he grabbed her hand, squeezing it tightly. To his surprise, she squeezed back just as tightly before slowly letting his hand go.

Her attention was fully on her photo album. Nora absentmindedly said, "You know, Stan, I'm so glad we met. You're such a good friend, so different from all the other guys. I really, really like you."

His heart was in his throat. What did she mean? "Nora, you said I'm different. How?"

She was still paging through her album, smiling at her memories. "I don't know how to say it, but you are just different from all the other guys. I don't have many guy friends. Well, actually you're the only one. Most boys are just, well, not into being friends. Boys never look at my face when they talk to me."

Nora bit her lip. Stan was having a hard time keeping his thoughts off how inviting those lips looked.

She continued, "The thing I like so much about you is you aren't like that. When you look at me, you always look into my eyes. And you listen without judging or telling me what to do. All my girlfriends do that and I hate it."

When she paused, Stan realized she was studying his eyes. She continued, "You share with me like you want me to know everything about you. I feel like I really know you and can talk to you about anything. You're special to me and I'm glad we're friends. I think you're the best friend of my entire life. So now you know why I like you. Why do you like me?"

Stan felt things were moving in the direction he wanted them to move. She had just said he was special, maybe like her best friend ever. What should he say? Should he tell her he'd been entranced with her since before he knew her name? Should he tell her what he really felt? That he was in love with her?

***

Stan's expression was impossible to read. He hadn't moved or said anything. Nora's heart started to shrivel in her chest. He appeared to be concentrating on her photos. Doubt entered her mind. She thought Stan really cared for her like she liked him, but he hadn't said a damned word. *I've got this wrong.* Maybe he didn't feel the warmth of their friendship like she did. *Stupid, stupid, stupid!* Her face flushed with embarrassment. She regretted saying anything at all. She needed to get up and away from him. Nora slowly closed her album and slid it back into her bookbag.

Stan suddenly seemed to come out of his trance. "Please don't put your pictures away. They're really good."

I'm such an idiot. Nora was so disappointed in herself that she'd said anything. Even though she was very popular, doubt about her own worth and why people liked her frequently tortured her. The group of girls she ran around with were cheerleaders—loud, rowdy and extremely shallow. That wasn't who she was and that was what had attracted her to Stan. He wasn't like that. *At least that's what I thought.* She knew she'd made a major mistake telling him she liked him.

She got up to leave. "I have to go now. I wish you a great weekend." Nora quickly fled the cafeteria.

***

Stan sat there in shock. Why hadn't he said anything? He cursed himself for being so stupid! Suddenly he became aware that the rest of the girls around the table were whispering with each other as they stared at him. His eyes got blurry as his face flushed. He ran to the hallway.

The weekend was miserable and lonely. Jeff was with his family in Chicago looking at colleges. Of course, Stan's parents were never home. He sat around the house debating what he should do. He decided to write Nora a note and put it in her locker on Monday morning, so she could read it before lunch.

This was the note he placed in her Algebra book:

Dear Nora,

    I'm sorry I didn't answer you when you asked if I liked you. I do, Nora, very, very much. You are my best friend, too. I really like the way you talk to me and share with me about your life, like your vacation and stuff. I think I hurt you and didn't mean to. I'm sorry that I got quiet when you told me how you felt. Your question took me totally by surprise. I didn't know what to say because my tongue was tied or I was tongue tied or something like that. Anyway, please give me another shot at our friendship. Love, Stan.

He debated on whether or not to write the second to last word, but he felt it.

His heart was in his throat when lunch period came around on Monday. *Will she still be mad?* Holding his tray, he looked for Nora, but she wasn't there. He sat at a table by himself and waited to see if she sat with her friends. She didn't show.

He was so disappointed that he barely made it to Thursday for lunch. He got his tray and looked for her, but again, she wasn't there. What was happening? Did she change her lunch period or was she avoiding him? He quickly wolfed down his meal before going to the library to see if she was there. She wasn't.

His heart was breaking. He hoped he hadn't made her mad. The pain in his chest made him desperate. After Science-Fiction class was over, he waited for Judy to leave. He tried to be cool as he walked down the hallway with her.

"Judy, I didn't see Nora this week. Is she okay?"

Judy gave him a puzzled look. "No, she's sick. Probably has mono from kissing her boyfriend." Judy turned toward him, looking for a reaction. He didn't give her one. "I plan on calling her tonight. Should I tell her you asked about her?"

Stan acted nonchalant. "No, just wondering. Kind of got used to sitting with her at lunch. I missed her, that's all."

Judy suddenly stopped, looking him in the eye. "Like oh my God, Stan, you're sweet on her, aren't you?"

Stan blushed and his voice rose an octave when he replied, "No, she's just my friend, Judy, you know?"

Judy read right through him. She shook her head as she frowned. "Stan, you better not be sweet on her. She's engaged and getting married in June. Did you know that? You'll just get hurt."

"I knew that," he lied. Suddenly he asked, "Do you know her address? I'd like to send her a get well card."

Judy gave him a doubtful look. "You're such a horrible liar."

"No, I'm not, Judy. I just wanted to send her a card, I swear!"

Her face softened. "Okay. She lives at 366 West Elm. I know she likes you, but only as a friend. Make sure you get that through your thick skull, Stanley. I like you too and don't want to see you get hurt. But sending her a get well card? She might like that. It might cheer her up." Judy turned to head to her World Cultures class.

Chapter 4

$\mathcal{K}$ aitlin could feel her pulse race, wondering if her heart would beat out of her chest. Jeremy quickly fell to his knees next to his father-in-law, placing his mouth over Stan's. He started providing breaths to keep the oxygen flowing to Stan's brain. Kelly was counting her chest compressions loudly enough to be heard in China.

The little one in Kaitlin's womb kicked sharply. *Beginning and end of life.* Kaitlin fought for control as she watched her husband and sister perform CPR on her daddy. A glimpse of movement caught her attention. Her mother entered the room.

Nora grabbed the wall to brace herself. Kaitlin's older sister Martina raced over to support their mother. Martina, always so cool under pressure in the courtroom was biting her lips to keep it inside. Kaitlin's gaze drifted to her mother. By the look on Nora's face, Kaitlin knew she understood what was happening and the gravity of the situation.

Tears tracked down her mother's face as she watched her family working hard to save the life of her husband of forty years. Kaitlin rushed over to hold Nora's hand. Together, Kaitlin and Martina propped her up.

The oldest sister, Cassandra, was on the phone with 911. As she spoke, she motioned for her daughter, Ellie, to go outside and wait for the ambulance.

Kaitlin jumped when she heard her mother's sob. "God, please don't take him. I need him. He's the love of my life! Guide their hands and be with this family. If we ever needed You, it's now!"

***

Stan couldn't get the thought of Nora out of his mind for the rest of the afternoon. Yes, he knew she was engaged, but he hadn't known she was getting married so quickly—three short months! In his mind, he knew he had to see her.

After school, Stan went home and dropped off his books. His mind formulated the plan. Despite Elm Street being a twenty-minute walk from his parent's house, Stan would pay Nora a visit. She might be engaged, but she wasn't married. Not yet. He had to tell her how he felt. Stan had to change her mind.

A strange, but cool idea came to him as he walked. As he passed one house with no cars out front, he detoured to the flowerbed. Stan quickly picked a couple of daffodils and three hyacinths. He walked until he came to Elm Street. The houses were large and fairly new. He finally found the Thomas home, very large and spacious. It was what people called a split level. He'd never seen a home so meticulously maintained or flowerbeds so beautiful.

He walked up to the front door, and raised his hand to knock. Suddenly he got cold feet. Nora was so wonderful and he was nothing, just a stupid guy from a poor family.

This is wrong. Let the girl alone. He turned to go.

Before he could leave the stoop, an icy voice rang out, "Hello, Stanley! What are *you* doing here?"

He spun around. Nora was standing in the doorway looking at him. She wasn't smiling. Her hazel eyes were smoldering.

"I asked you a question. What are you doing here, Stanley?"

Before he could speak, he glanced from her head to her toes. Nora had socks on and was wearing pajama bottoms. A pink housecoat was wrapped around her. Her eyes were pink and puffy and her hair was disheveled. She looked beautiful.

"I, uh, just wanted to see how you were doing. I hope you are feeling better. Are you?"

Her stare crushed his spirit. "Yes, I am feeling a little better than I was. Thank you, Stanley."

Please don't call me Stanley. He pulled the little bouquet from behind him and handed her his peace offering. She took it without smiling.

"I heard you had mono, so I wanted to bring you a get well bouquet."

He could see anger in her face. "Don't believe everything you hear," she said. "I do *not* have mono. It's the flu. Thanks for the flowers. Anything else you wanted?"

Stan could see her lips press together. "May I come in and visit with you for a while?"

"No. My parents aren't home and that would not be appropriate. I am going back inside before I catch a cold on top of the flu. Bye, Stanley."

This wasn't how he had hoped things would go at all. Sadly he said, "Goodbye, Nora." He turned away, but suddenly turned back. "Wait, Nora. *Please.* There's something else I wanted to say."

"What?" She looked irritated, but continued, "What else did you want to say?"

He squirmed a little before he answered. "Nora, you asked me a question last week and I didn't answer. If it's okay, I'd like to answer now and also explain why I didn't say anything right away. Can I?"

"You mean 'May I' and yes, you may, if it's quick."

"I'll try to hurry so you don't catch cold." He shifted his weight. "When you asked me the other day why I liked you, I couldn't answer right away because I didn't think you'd ever ask me that, not in a million years. Please don't think it was because I don't like you... I do, very, very much. More than you think, Nora." He stopped to gaze into her eyes. For a second he contemplated telling her he loved her, but Nora's expression hadn't changed. "I had a lot of friends at my old school, but very few here. And I've never had a girlfriend." Stan's cheeks heated. "I uh, mean a girl that was a close friend. And so you know, you're my closest and best friend, of all time. I'm sorry I didn't answer because I think it made you feel bad, didn't it?"

Her lips pinched together into a fine white line. "Yes, Stanley, you did hurt me, a whole lot. I'm fragile inside. I have what my counsellor calls a low self-esteem. Many of the girls who are my friends didn't become my friends until I started dating Bob. He was a big sports star—Mr. Popularity to everyone. He's the only reason I'm so popular now. Before, I was like you, just a girl adrift in a sea of students." She shook her head. "That didn't come out right. I didn't mean you were a girl, sorry about that."

For the first time, she smiled, slightly before her mouth again turned into a frown.

"Before Bob, I could count the number of friends I had on one hand. Now I have more than I know what to do with... but not a single one like you." She stopped and almost looked like she would cry.

"I never knew, Nora." Stan swallowed to buy himself more time. "I can't understand why anyone wouldn't like you. You are wonderful, at least to me. You're very pretty and kind. The day we actually met, you were the only one who was nice to me..." he looked away, "...when my zipper was down. The only one who treated me nice." He had to be careful here. Though he wanted to really tell her how he felt, and would soon, the timing wasn't quite right. He couldn't look in her eyes and tell her his true feelings, not right now.

Her eyes were moist. "Stan, one of the reasons I came to like you so much is that I feel I can talk to you about anything and everything. You never judge me or tell me what to do. You just listen and... what's the word? Oh yes, you *empathize*. That's right, you empathize with me. Sharing with you comes so naturally. And I think it works both ways. I told you things about me I haven't shared with any of my girlfriends—or even with my boyfriend because they would have made fun of me. And you always share so easily with me. I bet you've told me things no one else knows, haven't you?"

Stan nodded.

"I thought so. But then, when I asked you such a simple question, you didn't answer. I doubted our friendship, well really, I doubted myself. I began to think you weren't answering because you didn't really like me like I like you."

"Nora, that's not the case. I like you more than you know."

"Then why didn't you tell me, Stan?"

He blushed and studied her orange and white striped furry socks. "I don't know. I'm just stupid, I guess. I didn't know what to say, that's all. I was trying to find the right words, but couldn't. That's why I kept my big mouth shut. I'd give anything to go back and say the right thing."

For the first time, Nora fully smiled, and the kindness in her eyes made him feel better. "I wish you would have told me sooner," she said. "I really love your honesty and the openness we have. It hurt so much when it wasn't there. I felt so lonely. I missed you a lot, Stan. Next time, please don't leave me hanging, okay?"

Stan nodded again. "I put a note in your locker on Monday, telling you I was sorry."

"What? Carol brought home everything from my locker last night. I didn't see any note."

"I put it in your Algebra book."

Nora snickered. "That's the last place I would have looked! Why did you put it there?"

"That book was on top, that's why. I'm going to go now. I don't want you to catch a cold. I hope you feel better." Stan studied her eyes. "I hope my not answering you didn't hurt our friendship, did it?"

Her smile grew larger. "Not at all, Stan. Thank you for stopping by... and thank you for the beautiful flowers. That was very sweet." She bit her lip. "I know this might seem forward, but may I have your phone number? I will call you later, you know, just to make sure you get home okay. Would that be all right?"

Stan felt his eyes grow wide. He nodded.

Nora giggled at him. "By the way, I may not come to school next week. I have a doctor's appointment tomorrow and won't know until then if I can go back to school."

Stan kept nodding. He quickly pulled a piece of paper from his pocket, then jotted his number down. "Here. Call anytime, anytime at all."

Nora's expression turned serious as she reached for his hand, squeezing it tightly. "Stan, thank you for coming into my life. You are a godsend and you are also my best friend."

Stan ran home, but he wasn't sure if his feet touched the ground.

She called an hour later and they talked for hours, until her parents told her it was time for bed.

***

Nora couldn't get to sleep. There was a funny feeling in her chest. She smiled as she remembered her conversation with Stan. When he came over to make things right, her heart leaped for joy. He was so sweet.

But then another memory entered her mind. She remembered what transpired half an hour before he arrived.

She'd been watching *The Gong Show* on TV when the telephone rang. It was her fiancé, Bob. "Why are you calling this time of the day? Is everything all right? I thought you had a Philosophy class this afternoon."

His voice was very tense, "I did, Nora, but I cut class."

"Why? Is something wrong?"

A little delay followed. "I don't know. You tell me. Something wrong?"

She was puzzled. "I don't know. Why would you ask me that?"

"You remember Claire Sampson?"

Nora bristled. Of course she remembered that name. Claire had been Bob's steady until he met Nora. Nora suspected Claire had never given up hope on getting Bob back. Nora also suspected she still called him. And Nora believed Claire would do just about anything to come between them.

"Yes, Bob," she answered. "I remember her. Why is this important?"

"Because she called me today."

Nora's pulse quickened. So she *had* been right. "Why did she call you?"

"She's concerned, that's why."

"Concerned about what?"

"Concerned that my fiancée might have a new boyfriend. Some guy named Stan Jenkins."

Nora didn't know what to say.

Bob's voice softened. "Look, I know she's just a busy body, but is there any truth to this?"

Nora was confused. She loved Bob, but there was something about Stan that drew her to him. She had thought he was someone very, very special, but then last week when she asked him...

"Are you still there, Nora?"

"Yes, yes, I am, Stan."

"Stan?" Bob's voice was loud and angry. "You do remember my name is Bob, don't you?" Silence followed before he softly asked, "So is this Stan just a friend... or do I need to pay him a little visit to tell him to stay away from the girl I love?"

"No, please don't. He's just a kid and we're only friends, you know?"

Bob became even quieter when he said, "Nora, I'm sorry. It's just that I love you. I want to be with you forever, but being away from you at college and everything... sometimes it's hard." He hesitated briefly. "I want to ask you something and I really want you to tell me the truth. Are you having second thoughts about us getting married?"

"N-n-no. Why would you ask that?"

He sighed. "Nora, honey, I love you. I want you to be happy in life, more than anything else. If you decide it's not the time or if you change your mind, please tell me. I want you to be my wife, but more importantly than that, I want *you* to want to be my wife. If you have any doubts, it's only fair to tell me now."

"I told you I didn't. I gave my word, and besides, my parents made all the arrangements for the wedding. I couldn't let them or you down."

Bob sighed again, louder this time. "So you *are* having doubts. Listen, I want you to be sure. Don't worry about the money or that you gave me your word. This marriage—if we do get married—will be for life. If you have any doubts whatsoever, please, tell me now."

Nora answered, but not truthfully in her mind, "I don't have any doubts, Bob. I love you and want to be your wife. I really do. Please, don't bring this up again. When I said yes to you, I meant it."

They said goodbye. Then Nora spent the next half hour thinking about Stan, Bob and the futility of the whole situation. Did she love Stan? As she contemplated, she thought that out of all the people she had ever met, Stan was the nicest. In him, she knew she'd found her soulmate. Well, she had thought he was her soulmate.

If only he'd answered when she asked if he liked her.

Once again, she doubted herself and her worth. Maybe Stan hadn't answered because he really didn't care for her at all. That thought made her cry. Why did the friend she always dreamed about finally show up when her life was already in order—yes, in order—and planned? She decided she was through with Stan. Her life was in motion and she was ready. In twelve short weeks, she would be Mrs. Robert Patrick Crittendale.

And then she felt it. She'd sensed Stan standing outside her door.

She treated him coolly because she was angry with him. She had made up her mind she was through with him.

Then he explained why he hadn't answered. He told her that he liked her, much more than she could know. And by the look in his eyes, she already knew how much. Stan loved her. And suddenly she was honest with herself. She loved Stan, too.

She should keep him distant. My God, she was only ninety-five days away from her wedding day. But she couldn't stay away from Stan. She had to find out where this was going. Maybe Bob wasn't the one. Maybe she was meant to be with Stan.

After he had left, she cried in frustration. Did God send Stan her way as a blessing? Or was the devil just tempting her?

Sleep still didn't come. She relived the sweetness of their call that evening. When her mother reminded her it was time to head to bed, she almost told Stan she loved him.

When she finally drifted off to sleep hours later, she dreamed she was walking hand in hand on the beach in California. With her true love. Stan.

The doctor's appointment cleared her to return to school. She couldn't wait to see Stan at lunch. But first came her second-period class—Shorthand.

Nora took her seat and was getting out her steno pad. Miss Craley called her name. "Nora, I found this container of peanut brittle on my desk this morning with a note to give to you. Come up here, please." Miss Craley had a mischievous smile on her face. "Open it up, Nora, but mind your manners. You'll need to share it with the class." Miss Craley backed away.

Nora was standing at the front of the class. The steel can was cold and shiny. She grasped the lid and twisted. It didn't budge. She held it tightly in both hands, forcing the tips of her thumbs against the rim. It still wouldn't move. She held the can at arm's length to examine it. If finally dawned on her. The lid was cocked. Nora sat the cylinder on the desk and smacked her hand down to re-orient the cover. As soon as she did, the lid popped off, immediately followed by a bunch of spring-loaded snakes.

The class roared in laughter as Nora's face flushed.

Miss Craley was almost rolling on the floor, but above all, Nora heard raucous laughter coming from the hallway. She looked through the open door and saw Stan.

She ran into the hallway prepared to give him a piece of her mind. But Stan did something totally unexpected.

26

Out of sight from the rest of the class, he kissed her on the lips and looked into her eyes. Softly, so no one but Nora could hear, he uttered the words, "I love you!"

Then he quickly stole a second kiss and ran down the hall.

Nora stood there, watching him go. Her fingers touched her lips. She noticed how they tingled from Stan's touch.

When they met at lunch, they quickly reached for each other's hands. Nora no longer cared if anyone noticed. Everything had changed.

"My parents have dinner plans with friends tonight. We need to talk. Can you make it around seven?"

Stan smiled. "I can't wait." He squeezed her hand tightly before he left for his next class.

As she watched him walk off, her mind and heart argued. Nora was confused by her feelings, ending up a spectator to the internal battle. She loved Bob, of course, and it was a very warm and comforting love. But what she felt for Stan was different. While warm and comforting, it was also exhilarating. He was so much more than a guy she loved. He was her soulmate, the one God chose for her.

Nora had no idea what was going to happen, but her life, her future, her heart was right before her. She couldn't wait for seven o'clock.

Chapter 5

*K*aitlin held her mother's hand as they continued to watch Kelly and Jeremy perform CPR on Stan. It had been too long. The warmth was slowly draining out of Mama's hands. Thank God this had happened when the family was here. If nothing else, they were there to comfort her.

Kelly suddenly yelled, "I can't do this anymore. I need someone to take over." Almost as soon as she moved away, Kelly's husband Geeter took over chest compressions.

Kaitlin knew her sister must've broken his ribs with the force of her efforts. She'd heard them snap. If Daddy did survive, he'd have significant pain just from that. But it was slowly killing Kaitlin inside that he wasn't responding. This was a battle just to keep his blood and oxygen flowing to his brain until the paramedics arrived.

Martina's husband asked if Jeremy wanted him to take over, but Jeremy shook his head. Kaitlin knew Jeremy was in the best shape of anyone in the family and his stamina was excellent. The adrenaline probably bolstered Jeremy's resolve.

Time and time again, Stan's chest rose as Jeremy forced precious oxygen into his father-in-law's lungs. She studied Jeremy's eyes and saw the determination. He'd keep it up until he passed out.

Stan was not only her father, or the grandfather of their girls. Jeremy had often told Kaitlin what Stan meant to him. Stan had accepted Jeremy as his son a long time ago. Jeremy wouldn't leave a wounded comrade on the battlefield and he surely wouldn't give up on the man he loved as his father.

Kelly was sitting on a chair, arms wrapped around her knees as she watched the men's efforts. Kelly... the tough trauma nurse who could handle anything was losing it. *He's going to die. Kelly must sense it.* Kaitlin turned to Cassandra, "Where are the paramedics?"

"I-I-I don't know."

"Then call them again, now!"

Cassandra yelled into her phone, "Siri, get 911 on the line." As soon as she disconnected, the sounds of approaching sirens roared through the open front door. Kaitlin said a prayer of thanks when Ellie ran in, followed by the paramedics.

***

Nora heard the doorbell ring just before seven. Stan came in carrying another bouquet of flowers. "Hope you're not mad at me," he said handing them to her. "I shouldn't have told you how I felt or kissed you right there in the hall but I couldn't help myself."

Nora didn't respond, but smiled sweetly. He was blushing as he slowly reached for her hand. His hand was so warm. He gave her a long, soft kiss that made her entire body tingle. He started to pull away but Nora grabbed his neck, kissing him again softly and much longer this time.

Stan held her, his hands gently resting on her back. This was so different than Bob's embrace, because he always allowed his hands to roam much lower.

The kiss went on and on until Stan asked again, "Sorry I told you I loved you?"

Nora whispered in his ear, "No, Stan. I love you, too, but we have to talk. Let's figure this out." They sat side by side on the sofa as Nora poured out her feelings. "I love Bob, but that love is different than what we have. That love is more mature, knowing he wants to marry me. But I also love you... and the love I have for you is special and wonderful."

"I love you, too, Nora."

She could feel the warmth in her cheeks. She looked down. That's when she noticed something shiny—the engagement ring. *That ring means a commitment, not only to Bob, but to Mom and Dad.* She had given her word and promised herself to Bob. In the spot where her chest had tingled with anticipation a few minutes before, a dull ache now pounded.

She knew what she felt for Stan could not be. She had said yes, she had promised. Her heart was breaking. She stifled a sob.

He brushed her hair. "Why are you crying?"

"The way you make me feel is so wonderful. I love you so much, but it just can't be."

He looked confused. "Why not? I love you, do you understand that?"

"Yes, I do. I feel it too, but... I gave my word. It's not like Bob did anything wrong or that I'm not in love with him. Stan, in ninety-two days, I'll be his wife."

"Whoa, you might have to wait until I graduate, but I want to marry you, too!" Her tears intensified as he continued, "I will make you happy, Nora, just like you make me happy."

Inside, she knew it wouldn't work. She had to find some way to let him down easy. "Stan, I wish I would have met you before I met Bob. This thing... this thing between us can't work. No matter how much I wish it would, it just won't work."

Stan stiffened. "Why not? We have love, true love, Nora. I feel it. I know you feel it. Can you tell me otherwise?"

Her tears were blurring her vision. "No, I can't, but inside I know this is wrong. No matter how much I want you, we can only be friends. Nothing more. We can't go on like this. You can't kiss me or tell me you love me again."

Stan's face turned bright red. He stood, kicking the ottoman out of the way. "I understand. So, since he is graduating from college and asked you first, I'm left out in the cold? Or maybe it's because Bob's a famous football player, is that it? And no matter what you feel for me, he wins out. So you just want to be friends, is that right?"

Nora's heart was being torn from her chest, yet she nodded. It wasn't true that she wanted Bob because he played football. She wanted Stan, but she had made a commitment she must stick to.

He bristled and backed away. "Okay, I just want you to be happy. If it's friends you want, that's what we'll be."

Nora noted the pain in his eyes as he headed toward the door.

Stan didn't turn around as he said, "Goodbye, Nora," and closed the door quietly.

Nora cried herself to sleep that night. She worried how it would be at school. But when Thursday rolled around, Stan wasn't even there at lunch.

She asked Julie if he'd been in school that day. Julie said he was. So Nora looked for him the following Monday, but Stan still didn't come to the cafeteria. She tried to call him that night and many nights afterwards, but he never answered his phone. Nora knew if they did talk, she would tell him she had changed her mind. There was nothing she wanted more in life than to be with Stan, to have a life with him... but he had disappeared. She didn't see him again in school.

Graduation came and went. In mid-June, Nora married Bob. She knew she'd hurt Stan and wished they could talk, but he had obviously distanced himself. She missed him so much. A portion of her felt like she was dying.

Shortly after their wedding, Bob took a job in Birmingham, Alabama, where they set up house in an apartment. Nora slowly let go of the feelings she had for Stan. As their marriage progressed, she found that her feelings for Bob took the place of Stan in her heart.

Bob turned out to be a great husband. He was kind, considerate, loving. He eventually became her soulmate. Bob's job took them to Denver, then Boston and finally to Baltimore. He was very successful.

In the third year of their marriage, she gave him a little girl, Cassandra. Two years later, she gave him a second daughter, Martina. Life was total bliss for her, for a while. She had almost forgotten Stan. Almost, but not completely.

***

Stan held it together until he was out of Nora's door. He ranted the whole way home, cursing God, everyone and everything he knew because he couldn't be with the girl he loved. Nora only wanted to be friends, but Stan needed her for more than that. He loved her. He needed her, so much more than she would ever know. In his mind, he tried to figure out how to be her friend only, but couldn't do it. He would screw it up. He would tell her he loved her again. He would cause her pain.

So he did the honorable thing. He disappeared from her life.

School ended as an empty husk. He had no friends. Even Jeff became distant. Life at his parents' house was lonely and filled with sadness. If he saw his mother or father for more than one or two hours a week, that was a lot. He had been taking care of himself since he was twelve. That was the year of the big argument between his parents.

His house had never been filled with love but one autumn day, he came home to hear his parents screaming at each other. As he listened, he slowly understood his mother had been having an affair.

Stan's parents had met when his mom was a sophomore in college. His dad worked as a machinist in an automotive factory. She had told her husband time and time again that she had to give up her future and all chance for happiness because she became pregnant with Stan. Sometimes, she would openly blame Stan for her lot in life.

As he listened to them fight, Stan wondered why they just didn't split up, like some of his friends' parents did. Over the years, it became obvious they didn't love each other. Their marriage became openly hostile. Perhaps they knew by staying together, they could torture one another.

It also tortured Stan. He became withdrawn, losing all of his friends. In his mind, he pretended he was in a loving home. He wanted to find the perfect woman and have the perfect family. He vowed to God above he would never treat his children like he'd been treated. He would never let a day go by without letting them know how much they were loved. When he would marry and have children, their home would be filled with love.

After his parent's big blowout, Stan's father turned to drinking. At first he would drink at home. When he drank beer, he was jolly. But when he hit the hard stuff, he would become violent, often directing that violence at his son.

Stan learned to stay away from him. His father must have realized what he was doing because he ceased coming home on a regular basis. Instead, he'd go to the bar after work and stay gone all night long.

His drinking brought trouble at work. When Stan was fourteen, his dad got fired. He was able to get other employment, but he would always go on drinking binges and lose job after job.

Stan's parents finally lost their large modern home and moved into the little run down rancher they rented during his last two years of high school.

While his father turned to liquor, his mother turned to men. Often Stan would come home to find strangers in the house. One day when he was fifteen, he saw a man slap his mother. That was too much and Stan attacked him. The man beat Stan until he was unconscious. After that, his mother took her affairs elsewhere. This resulted in Stan having the run of the house all the time. He cooked for himself. He washed his own clothes. He did the dishes. He learned how to survive.

After Nora told him she only wanted to be friends, Stan became even more of a hermit. With no one to turn to, he dove into books. His mind became a sponge. He read everything he could find with a passion. That satisfied him for a little while, but still he grew restless.

After Nora married, he took a job in a garage down the street, starting out by pumping gas. Over the summer, they allowed him to start working on cars. Stan found he had a gift for things mechanical. By the end of the summer, he was rebuilding engines in the garage.

Stan thought about Nora a lot. She was the only girl he ever dreamed of, but it wasn't meant to be. He actually attended her graduation. He considered going up to see her afterwards, but this very large man swept her in his arms. It must have been her fiancé. In his mind, he said goodbye to her, for good.

Stan took the SATs in October and was surprised to find he had the highest score in school history. Suddenly, colleges were contacting him about attending their campuses. However, he had no money and didn't bother telling his parents.

On his eighteenth birthday, he enlisted in the Army. Graduation came and his parents didn't even attend the ceremony. He boarded a train for boot camp the very next day without even saying goodbye. He never saw his mother or father alive again.

***

Stan was tightening the bolts to put the manifold back on the tank engine. *I am blessed.* He loved being a tank mechanic. He enjoyed his deployment at the large NATO base along the West German border, near East Germany. In the Army, he found friends—lots of friends. He even met a few women, but wasn't serious about any of them.

While he loved working with his hands, his mind kept going to the future. If he ever had the family he craved, being a mechanic wouldn't give him the way of life he wanted to provide for his family. So he saved every penny he earned, investing it wisely. He also took advantage of the Army's educational opportunities, slowly racking up college credits for when he discharged.

"Sarge?"

Stan looked up to see Private Able in front of him. "Yes?"

"Message from the CO. He wants you in his office, now. Double-time." The kid looked scared. He'd only arrived the previous day. "His words, not mine, Sarge."

Stan washed up and found his way to the Commander's office. He stood at attention and announced himself to the aide, "Jenkins here. Reporting as ordered."

Stan had dealt with this man before, a second lieutenant. All business, all the time. But Stan noted something amiss in his reaction. "At ease, Jenkins. I'll inform the CO."

The lieutenant disappeared into the next room. Almost instantaneously, he returned with Major Parker.

Stan had worked for Parker for two years now. He couldn't recall seeing the current expression on his supervisor's face before.

"Come in, Stan. Take a seat."

The hair on the back of Stan's neck stood at attention. Parker never called anyone by their first name.

Stan sat, facing his CO. Parker studied him briefly before looking out the window. "Hate this part of the job." He turned his head, locking his eyes on Stan's. "Just got word from stateside. Sorry to tell you this, but your mother died two days ago."

Things became a little blurry as Stan drew in a sharp breath. "How'd she die, sir?"

"Killed in a car accident. I'm sorry. Were you close?"

"No. Didn't have a good relationship with either parent. Dad's an alcoholic. She ran around on him. They only stayed together to torture each other. I was stuck in the middle. It was a miserable existence. I was basically on my own from the time I was twelve. Cooked, cleaned, all that stuff by myself."

"Sorry. I'm giving you leave to go home. You have four weeks built up. Take what you need."

Stan stood. "Thank you, sir."

Parker's face clouded. "Again, I'm sorry for your loss and what you went through."

"I'm not. My parents taught me a valuable lesson. They taught me how *not* to treat your children. Can guarantee you, sir, I won't pass that pain on to the children I'll have someday. I want their lives to be perfect."

Parker studied him. "Stay positive, Stan. Hope things work out that way."

"I *will* make it happen, sir."

"I believe you. You're dismissed, Sergeant."

Stan returned stateside long enough to attend the funeral. His father must've been too liquored up to show up for either the viewing or the funeral. Stan was the only one in attendance.

One hour after he buried her, Stan was on his way back to Germany. Six short weeks later, his CO called him in again to tell him that his father had died of an alcohol overdose. Stan made a second return stateside to bury his father. Again, he was the only one in attendance. After settling his father's estate, Stan donated the little bit of money left over to Alcoholics Anonymous.

Back in Europe, Stan excelled in all things. He was placed in command of a small platoon of mechanics. He loved leading people.

When his four-year hitch was almost up, Parker called him into his office. Stan was escorted in by the lieutenant. Parker pointed to a chair. "At ease, Jenkins. I see your enlistment is almost up."

"Yes, sir. Three weeks left."

"You've excelled at leading your men. This army needs good men like you. How about re-enlisting? But this time, you'll go directly to Officer's Candidate School."

Stan smiled. "Thank you, sir. I appreciate the offer, but I don't plan on staying. I've got seventy-five college credits racked up. I've already been accepted at Penn State University. Plan on pulling a double major—chemistry and business management."

Parker nodded. "Sounds like you've got a good plan."

"Yes, sir. Don't know if you remember, but I once told you I wanted my children's lives to be perfect. Step one, sir. This is step one of my plan."

Chapter 6

*N*ora saw it clearly. *This is it. The end.* She'd somehow made it through the loss of her first husband, Bob. She didn't know if she had the strength to go through it a second time. If Stan died, her life would be over. Stan was everything, her entire world. The thought of life without him broke her heart in two. Again, she petitioned heaven, *If you need to take one of us, God, take me. Please don't leave me behind.*

Finally, the paramedics were in the room. Kelly came alive, talking non-stop, telling them what meds her dad was on, when he last ate, and describing their efforts to bring him back. The paramedics encouraged Geeter and Jeremy to keep CPR going while they hooked monitors up to Stan. When they were ready, they ordered them to stop. Jeremy's hands were shaking. Kaitlin's cheeks were wet as she held Nora's hand tightly while they watched the paramedics work.

"I've got a shockable rhythm," said one of the EMTs. "Everyone, stand clear!"

Nora watched them shock him once, twice... and finally a third time. On the third try, the other paramedic yelled, "I have a pulse!"

They lifted Stan onto a stretcher and wheeled him out.

***

Just as he had in the Army, Stan excelled during his time at Penn State. He made Dean's list every semester and managed a 4.0 GPA.

Stan became attracted to a grad student who worked in the chemistry lab. She had a southern accent and was a little heavy set, but oh those bright blue eyes.

One evening he finally worked up the courage to talk to her. "Excuse me, ma'am. I hope I'm not being forward, but you're in here all the time, so, I, uh, wanted to introduce myself. Stan Jenkins," he said, extending his hand.

She shot him a playful smirk. "Congratulations."

What? "I'm sorry. Congratulations for what?"

She couldn't hide her smile. "For finally introducing yourself."

"Oh, well, I mean..."

"So... Did you want to know my name, too?"

Stan could feel the blush in his cheeks. "That was my objective, really."

She broke out in a happy laugh and extended her own hand. "Linda Pruitt. For weeks I've been wondering if you would ever talk to me."

Stan didn't get the chance to finish his experiment because of their conversation. Linda was from Knoxville. Her father was the Physics chair at University of Tennessee. Her mother was the CEO for a large electronics manufacturing firm. Stan found out she was an only child, one year younger than him. That first night was the beginning of their relationship. They grew close, occasionally catching dinner together.

One cold January evening in his last semester, Stan was the only student left in the chemistry lab as he worked on an extra credit project. It was nice and warm inside, but outside, it was snowing heavily.

Linda stopped in, a troubled look on her face.

"Something bothering you, Lin?"

"You see how bad it's snowing?"

Stan shrugged. "Yes. Are you concerned about getting to your room?"

"I live off campus."

"I could give you a lift."

Her smile was awesome. He thought she might live in one of the university dorms, but she directed him onto a state highway toward Seven Mountains. Just before the turn to the summit, she directed him up a paved road that snaked its way up to the top. Sitting there in the almost blinding snow was a beautiful chalet. Linda invited him in.

"You live here?" Stan asked.

She nodded with a smile.

"Wow! Either Penn State pays very well or you're connected," he said, following her in the front door.

She kicked off her shoes as she walked to the hearth. Within seconds, a warm fire lit the room. "Wanted something cozy. Got a little over five thousand square feet. Like it?"

"It's beautiful. Do you really live here? This place is something else."

She studied his eyes. "Yep. Bought and paid for. Make yourself comfy."

Stan couldn't help but stare at the house and its adornments.

Linda linked her arm in his. "Let me give you the grand tour." For the next half hour, they took in her antiques and collectibles.

Stan was suspicious. "I still can't believe all this is yours. How can you afford this place?"

She simply smiled as she put on a pot of coffee. "Stan, you are the only one who I ever shared this with. Everyone else thinks I'm dumpy, just another penniless grad student. It never ceases to amaze me the way most people treat me. If they knew what I was worth, they'd bow down like I was a queen." She walked over to study his face. "That's the reason I like you. You've always been so nice to me, not because I had money, but just because you like me. My grandfather made a fortune in the stock market. When he passed away, I received a large inheritance. I only work because I want to. Truth be told, I'm one of the richest women in the state."

"I had no idea."

Her smile was enchanting. "I know that. Thirsty, Stan?"

He nodded.

She returned from the kitchen with a large Brandy snifter. "My hobby's photography. Here's an album from my cruise through the Panama Canal last year."

Stan paged through, but it stirred a sad memory. Long ago, someone he had loved had shown him her photo album. *Wonder where Nora is now. Hope she's happy in life.*

Linda must have caught the glimpse of sadness. She leaned over and gently kissed him. She smiled, taking his hand so they could snuggle on the couch. Stan didn't return to his apartment that night.

Life at Penn State suddenly became wonderful for Stan. Most nights were spent at Linda's mountaintop retreat. As May approached, Stan decided it was time to talk about the future. "I love you, Linda. Do you think someday we should get married?"

Much to his surprise, Linda gave him a warm kiss. "Why wait? Let's get married as soon as you graduate."

Ten days after graduation, they wed at her parents' Baptist church in Knoxville. Despite Stan's protest at using her money, they enjoyed a three-month honeymoon in the South Pacific. Life was bliss. Stan's dreams were finally coming true.

Returning to State College, Stan took a job as a chemist with a small chemical company in nearby Bellefonte. He had been in the job for two years when Linda asked him to have a seat.

"Stan! Guess what?" Her excitement was contagious.

"I don't know, what?"

"I accepted a position at UCLA. Isn't that great?"

Stan stared at her in disbelief. "What? I didn't even know you put in for that position. May I ask why?"

She sighed. "I want a change. There's not much to do here anymore, besides watching Joe Paterno coach football. I'm tired of long, cold, snowy winters. It's time to leave Pennsylvania and move to the land of the sun. I am going to California. Want to come?"

Stan was totally floored. "*Do I want to come?* You never mentioned moving anywhere, let alone to California. Didn't you think you might want to discuss something like this with me, your husband?"

She looked puzzled. "Since when do I have to okay what I want to do with you? You might be my husband, but you aren't my boss."

"Lin, please don't take it that way. I'm not trying to boss you. But you aren't the only one who has things going on here. Just deciding to up and move across the country affects me, too."

She sneered at Stan, which bothered him. "If you're talking about that rinky dink little job you have, don't worry about it. I have more than enough money that neither of us will ever have to lift a finger again. Just don't smother me."

She stood, looking down on him.

"That's why I asked whether you want to come with me," she said. "If you do, great. If not, we'll work it out somehow. But we're individuals. Do whatever you want. I was planning on selling the cabin, but if you want to stay, I'll keep it." With that, she walked away.

Of course, Stan would go with her. He just wished she had communicated a little better; that was all he wanted.

Stan gave his two-week notice at work the following day. He loved State College, but Linda was his wife. He didn't ever want to fight with her. He had seen enough fighting between his own parents.

Within a month, they relocated to California. After they were settled in, Linda started her job. She worked long hours. Being a stay at home husband wasn't in Stan's genes, though. He applied for several positions.

His third interview was at California Polymers. They had several openings and Stan applied for a research and development chemist position. When he arrived for the interview, a gentleman named Joe Summers took him into the conference room.

The man reviewed Stan's resume then asked, "Did you serve in the Army in Germany supporting tanks?"

That was a weird question. "Yes sir, I did. I was there almost four years."

"I thought that was you!" Joe beamed.

Stan looked hard at the man. His face was not familiar. "I'm sorry. Do I know you?"

Joe laughed. "Nope. We've never met, but my son Kyle served under you. He has a different last name—Kyle Brubaker. Remember him?"

Stan thought back and quickly remembered. Kyle was a young soldier who had gotten into trouble with the West German police. He had been caught fooling around with a young girl. The problem was that the girl in question was the daughter of a police officer. Of course, the police wanted to press charges but Stan intervened. He finally negotiated a deal to rebuild the officer's engine in return for all charges being dropped.

"Yes, I remember Kyle. How's he doing?"

"Fine. He married Bertrana and they have two children. Thanks for getting him off." Very little interviewing was done after that point. The two shared service stories for a while before Joe said, "I don't think this is the job for you."

Stan's hope tumbled.

Joe continued, "Any man who goes out on a limb to protect those who work for him has excellent leadership skills. I have a section head management position available in the R&D department. I'd like to offer that position to you instead."

Stan accepted and for the time he lived with Linda in California, his job went well. Under his leadership, California Polymers increased their market share by launching an average of ten new products a month. Stan accumulated ninety-one patents to his credit.

Stan and Linda had a fairly decent life, though they both worked long hours. One thing really bothered him, though. They quarreled about their future. Stan wanted a family, but Linda was never ready.

As time went on, he began to grow disillusioned with their relationship. It seemed Linda was only interested in Linda. She did what she wanted, when she wanted, and with whom she wanted. Occasionally she would disappear for a couple of days without warning. Sometimes she would ask him to go along, but other times she didn't even invite him. Stan thought maybe she just needed her space, so he bit his tongue. True, they had some wonderful vacations and time together, but as time went on, they grew apart. Stan wanted a child, hoping it would bring back the closeness. But every time he brought it up, an argument followed.

One May weekend, the discussion came to a head. "Linda, can we talk about having children?"

She looked at him and sighed, "Stan, let me make this clear. I don't want to have children with you."

Her words shocked him, but it was the tone of her voice that disturbed him most. "You don't want to have children? Or you don't want to have children *with me*?"

She eyed him and shook her head. "Actually, neither of those sounds like a good choice. I like my life, just as it is. I don't want a kid tying me down. I've told you this time and time before. I think I need a change."

Stan was getting very concerned. "What do you mean?"

She brushed his hair out of his eyes and sadly smiled. "I guess I've been spoiled. I'm used to getting my way. That doesn't really fit into the way of life you want, does it?"

Stan slowly shook his head.

"I need to be honest with you," she said. "I'm not happy in our relationship anymore."

Stan slowly began to understand. "You don't love me anymore, do you?"

"Not really..."

"There's someone else isn't there?"

Linda bit her lip. "Yes. I've been seeing Al for about a year. I used to love you, but I don't anymore. I'm in love with him and want to marry him. I think the time has come for us to part ways."

As they discussed the end of their marriage, it became clear to Stan that she was more interested in finding a way to keep as much of her money as she could. California was a no-fault state, so half of her fortune would be his.

In the five years of their marriage, he had never asked about her finances. Now, she reluctantly told him how rich of a man he was going to be.

Stan was disgusted. "I married you for love, not money. It's clear to me your fortune means more to you than I ever did. You can keep every damned penny."

Linda looked so relieved. "Don't think of it that way, Stan. I did love you, but sometimes I just need a change in life. This is one of those times."

Stan cleaned out his things that evening, then rented a small apartment the next day. But California no longer appealed to him.

To his surprise, shortly after he and Linda decided to call it quits, California Polymers announced a merger with another chemical company. Stan stopped by Joe's office. "Hey, Joe."

"There's Stan. I was just going to call you." Joe slapped him on the shoulder. "You heard about the merger? We'll be moving R&D operations to their lab. Much bigger, newer and more spacious. It's also close to our biggest customers. We discussed this at the board meeting last night. They decided they want *you* to head it up, but you'd have to move there."

Stan's heart rate increased. "Where's there?"

"Motor City. Detroit. How'd you like to be the Operations Manager for us? Of course, you'll want to talk to Linda about it first."

Stan quickly considered the position. Detroit wasn't his first—or even in his top fifty choices of locations—but he wanted out of California.

"Tell me more, like how rich you're going to make me."

Joe smiled. "Come on in and let's chat."

Stan relocated to Detroit in late August.

Chapter 7

*N*ora and her daughters arrived at the hospital shortly after the ambulance backed in. The men had stayed behind to tend to the children. Kelly checked in with the triage desk, asking about Stan's condition. Nora noted she wiped her eyes several times before returning.

"What did they say, Kelly?"

Her daughter's eyes didn't meet hers. "Daddy coded twice on the way here and had to be revived. He's in the cardiac intensive care unit undergoing evaluation." Kelly was having trouble not breaking down and she was the strong one, used to medical emergencies all the time.

Nora knew the nightmare was getting worse. Kelly turned to her, but had to turn away. *My daughter's afraid.* Stan wasn't going to make it. *I can't live without him, God. Please.* Tears ran down her cheeks. As she looked around the room, there wasn't a dry eye. Cassandra was praying out loud, asking everyone to join hands.

From inside of Nora, something welled up. *This isn't how Stan would want us to act.* Nora cleared her throat. "Daddy wouldn't want us to sit here and cry. Instead, he'd want us to remember the good times, to cheer each other up. I want everyone to share their favorite memories of Dad."

Nora watched her daughters exchange glances. *They think I've lost my mind.* Eventually, Cassandra stood and dried her eyes. "I'm the oldest, so I'll go first. My favorite memory of Daddy goes way back to before you married him, Mom. It was that first year when he was babysitting while you were waitressing. For Christmas, I wanted a Cabbage Patch doll so badly. I didn't tell you because even at that age, I knew money was tight. He took Tina and me shopping to buy your gifts. We went into the city, downtown. After shopping for you, he took us to an elegant restaurant and let us order dessert. Daddy let us skip the meal but made us promise not to tell you."

Nora patted Cassandra's hand. "Just like your dad. He always spoiled all of you. Kindest man I ever met." Kaitlin was sitting next to her and held her other hand.

Cassie continued, "After that wonderful dessert, he took us to a toy store and asked us to show him what we wanted Santa to bring. I picked out a couple of games and the prettiest Cabbage Patch doll I ever saw." She sobbed hard for a second before dabbing at her eyes. "And on Christmas morning, everything I'd picked out was under the tree. Santa came through, but I now know it wasn't Santa, it was Daddy. And even though he wasn't even there that Christmas Day, he made sure all of us were happy."

Nora wiped her eyes. "I remember. Stan stopped by very late Christmas Eve. He had gifts for both of you, but refused to tell me what they were. And I didn't even know he had brought other gifts from Santa. On Christmas morning, I was ashamed because I couldn't afford to get you anything from Santa, but there were gifts under the tree from him. And the look on your faces when you opened them was priceless. I had no clue how Daddy knew, but I guess I do now. The reason he didn't stop by on Christmas morning was because Tim was coming over. That was how your father was... always caring more about others than himself."

Kaitlin said through her tears, "Momma, don't talk like Daddy won't make it through. He will. You have to believe that."

Nora nodded, but the hope in her heart was fading.

***

Stan found the challenges of his new position exhilarating and it took his mind off the impending divorce. He worked long shifts, sometimes as many as sixteen-hour days. Stan found himself living off take-out and occasionally, better quality restaurant food.

Several of his chemists raved about a place called Xavier's Greek Restaurant. Stan decided to give it a try one evening. The enticing aroma of the food whetted his appetite. Stan was quickly seated. Famished, everything on the menu looked great. He was debating what to order when the waitress came over. Engrossed in the menu, he failed to look up.

"Stan?" the waitress suddenly asked. "Are you Stanley Jenkins?"

Stan looked up and did a double take! Standing before him was Nora Thomas. Or was she Nora Crittendale now?

"Nora! Is that really you?"

She nodded.

Stan stood up and hugged her. She looked very tired, but she was so much prettier than he remembered. "What are you doing here?"

"I work here. What are you doing here? Do you still live in Detroit?"

"I just moved back a little while ago. I manage the big plastics plant. Never thought I'd see you again! You're even more beautiful than I remember. I figured you'd be a stay at home mother. Maybe I'm being a little forward. Do you have children?"

Her bottom lip quivered. "Yes, two little girls, ages five and seven. How about you? You have children?"

He smiled sadly. "No, not yet. Someday. How's married life?" As soon as he asked, he regretted it because her eyes teared.

"I'm... I'm not married anymore. I'm a widow. Cancer took Bob two years ago."

Stan looked at her left hand and saw an engagement ring.

Nora followed his eyes and said, "Yes, I recently got engaged to a wonderful man. He was Bob's co-worker and his best friend. We're getting married next April."

Stan's heart dropped. Of all the rotten luck!

"How about you," she asked. "Are you married?"

Technically he still was, so he replied, "Yes. My wife's back in California. She works at UCLA."

Her boss walked by. "Keep it moving, Nory! I don't pay you to socialize."

She gave Stan a sad smile. "Sorry. May I take your order?"

Stan asked for the ribeye then watched her walk away. In his mind, his thoughts drifted back to high school and their last kiss. He remembered the softness of her lips and the wonderful enticement of her body close to him.

He was still lost in that memory when she delivered his food. Before he could ask Nora anything else, she got called away to another table. She dropped his check off later, asking him if he enjoyed his food. He said it was great, but in reality, he couldn't remember the taste... or even what he had ordered. His every thought had been focused on Nora.

Stan quickly became a regular, always asking to be seated in Nora's section. Over the next two weeks, he discovered she had off on Monday and Friday evenings. He made sure to eat at the restaurant every day she worked. He always left her a twenty-dollar tip, which she thanked him for. But when he came in on the Wednesday of the third week, she looked preoccupied and angry.

As she brought him his 'regular' dessert of Coconut Cream pie (she brought it automatically and he didn't even have to order it anymore), he asked, "Everything all right, Nora? You seem a little, how should I say it, distressed."

She dabbed her eyes with a tissue. "Times are a little rough right now. First, my old car broke down, then my sitter tells me she's scaling back. She can only watch the girls one night a week starting next week. I don't know what to do. I need this job. I can't make ends meet without it and I have no idea how I'll be able to afford to get the car fixed."

"What's wrong with the car?"

"I don't know. When I turn the key, it just clicks and won't start."

"Oh, that's a simple fix. Sounds like either the battery or the voltage regulator is bad."

Her eyebrows raised. "You can tell that based on what I just told you?"

"Um-huh."

She looked even more distressed. "How much will that cost?"

He took a sip of his coffee. "Oh, that depends." He saw fear in her eyes.

"Depends on what?"

"Depends on whether you take it to a high priced garage or whether you have a friend who knows a little something about cars."

She shook her head. "I don't have any friends anymore, what with my life being work and the girls. And I surely don't know anyone who fixes cars."

Stan smiled broadly. "Hmm. I think I know someone who might be able to help you out."

Her eyes opened wide. "Really? Would he charge much?"

He shook his head.

She slowly smiled. "It's you, isn't it, Stan?" He nodded. "I didn't know you knew how to fix cars!"

He pushed his chair back and laughed, "Well, I worked on tanks in the Army, so I think I can find my way around a car's engine compartment."

She looked around. It was a slow night with no customers in her section. Nora sat down and stared at him in wonder.

Stan reached across to pat her hand. "Let's get a couple of things straight. First, you do have friends, at least one and that's me. Second, anytime you need anything, just ask. Now, I have a question for you."

She gave him a warm smile. "What's that?"

"How'd you get to work today?"

Her smile vanished. "I took a taxi. I had to drop the girls off at the sitter first before coming to work."

"I see. How will you get home?"

"I'll have to do the taxi thing again. They are so expensive! When do you think you can fix my car? Tonight?"

"It won't be tonight. First, I need to troubleshoot it. Then I'll need to get parts. Probably be at least three days because the auto parts stores around here all seem to close at five."

"Great," she said sarcastically. "All my tips will go for taxi service."

"That's too bad. If there was just some way to get you a car... you know... one that might be able to carry your girls." He rubbed his chin as he stared off into space. "I'd loan you my Corvette, but that probably isn't very safe."

Her eyes opened wide. "You have a Corvette?"

"'Sixty-nine Stingray. You *could* borrow it if you wanted."

"Stan, that's very generous, but like you said, what about the girls? And what would you drive?"

"Oh, I could drive my other car."

"You have two cars? How much do you make?"

Stan laughed. "I did tell you I am the Operations Manager, didn't I? That means I'm the boss and they pay me quite well—enough to support two cars. I have an idea. What would you say if I loaned you my second car? It has a big back seat and will be safe for your girls."

She blushed, shaking her head. "That's very generous, but that would be an imposition. I couldn't, really."

He frowned. "May I ask you something?"

"Of course."

"Do you consider me to be your friend?"

A smile slowly lit up her face. "Yes, Stan, I do. Ever since we were kids."

"And friends help each other out, right?"

She started to laugh, pointing her finger at him. "I see where you're going with this but..."

"And when you have a friend, you bend over backwards not to offend them, right?"

"I suppose, but..."

"So why risk offending me by saying no?" He smiled, then looked at her meaningfully. "Seriously, my other car just sits there. I only planned on using it during the winter because I won't be able to drive the Vette. You'd actually be doing me a favor. Please reconsider."

She thought for a minute before responding, "How much will this cost me? I won't take charity."

He contemplated for a few seconds. "Do you work on Saturday?"

"I do in the morning, but I get off at one. Why?"

"How about a home-cooked meal on Saturday night?"

The gruff sound of her boss's voice interrupted them. "Nory, customers in your section. Think you can give them a little attention, too?"

Nora glanced in Stan's direction briefly before heading off to wait on the new table. Stan watched her from a distance, admiring the way her eyes smiled as she spoke with the customers. Though she tried to hide it, she was also keeping an eye on him. When she realized he'd caught her gaze, she blushed.

She returned to Stan's chair with a coffee pot. "Need a refill?"

Stan covered his cup with his hand. "What about that home-cooked meal?"

She studied his face before whispering, "Wouldn't your wife be upset?"

Stan thought that Linda wouldn't care less—but he couldn't tell Nora that. "Absolutely not. She has male friends and gets together with them all the time. It's no big deal, unless you don't want me to come over. If you don't, I understand."

Nora bit her lip. "I guess that would be okay. Please don't expect anything elaborate. I am on a very tight budget."

"Campbell's soup and toasted cheese sandwiches would be fine."

Nora smiled at him. "I think we can do that."

"Tell you what, I have a few errands to run. What time do you get off?"

"Ten. Why?"

"I'll be back before ten, then we'll go get my other car. Better yet, can I have your address? That way I can drop my Vette off at your place. Then you can get used to the other car. Deal?" He extended his hand. She searched his face. She reached for his hand and shook it. The feel of her hand in his started a spark inside him. *Dammit, she's engaged.*

"Deal! Here's your check." Nora wrote down her address. She left to return to her other table.

Stan paid the bill, slipping two twenties in as a tip. On the back of his check, he wrote:

> This should cover your taxi ride from earlier. Your one and only friend (guess that means best friend), Stan. ☺

Stan drove his Corvette to Nora's apartment complex and found a pay phone to call a cab. Arriving back at his apartment, he grabbed the keys to his second car. He then drove to a gas station, filling the tank completely so Nora wouldn't have to worry about it. Life might be rough for Nora, but Stan planned on smoothing some of the rough edges.

Chapter 8

$\mathscr{N}$ora needed to find the good within the bad, something Stan taught her. *Always be the example.* She would set the stage.

While all her daughters were struggling, the strain was showing hardest on Kelly.

Nora patted her daughter's hand. "I want you to go next. You were always special to Daddy."

Kelly wiped her cheeks and took a moment to compose herself. "I think my favorite memory of Daddy was when I was about ten. I loved softball so much, remember?" All her sisters nodded. "It was my birthday and I wanted all of us to play ball that day, but it was pouring rain. I'd been looking forward to it so much. Then sometime after midnight, Daddy woke me up. Outside, a beautiful full moon lit up the yard. All of you were waiting on me. Neighbors must have thought we were nuts, carrying on like that. But that was my wish... and he made it come true. He always had a way of making my dreams come true."

Nora hugged Kelly. Talking about it had helped. She was no longer crying.

A male voice surprised her. "I'd like to go next, Mom, if that's okay." It was Jeremy.

Everyone turned to find Geeter and Jeremy standing there.

Nora's eyes blurred. *My sons have come.*

"I thought you two were home with the kids," Kelly cried.

"Ellie's got everything under control. Had the kids eating out of her hand. She told us to come be with her Mimi."

Kelly and Kaitlin ran to their husbands, holding them tightly.

Nora's heart lifted at their arrival. Her eyes met Jeremy's. He had worked so hard to get them all to this point. His eyes were red.

She reached to hold his hand. "Yes, go ahead."

"My favorite memory of Dad was the first birthday I celebrated with Kaitlin after we were married. Of course, it was a girls' day out and I was missing her. Dad took me into his workshop. We spent the afternoon building a crib for our future children. I'd never worked with wood before and he took the time to explain everything. Later on, he took me out to a ball game. That was the day I realized he had filled the hole in my chest when my own father died. Without a word, I knew he considered me his son."

Jeremy's breath was measured, as if he was trying to control it. He was trying to be strong, just like Stan. His wife comforted him.

Nora whispered silently, "You did this. The love surrounding me right now is because of you. Don't you dare leave me."

***

Nora kept checking her watch. Would he really do what he said? Out of all the restaurants in Detroit, he showed up at hers and sat in her section. Was this a sign or another temptation? *You know my inner thoughts, hopes and dreams, Lord. I leave it all up to You.*

Just before Nora took off her apron for the night, Stan walked in, sitting at the counter while he waited. Her heart beat so loudly she could barely hear anything else. Nora walked over to pat his hand.

"Stan, this is really nice of you. You didn't have to do this."

He offered her a smile that made her knees weak. "Oh, it's nothing you wouldn't do for me!"

"Somehow, I don't think so. You went further than I ever could have. Thank you!"

She clocked out and collected her tips. Stan stood, smiled, and opened the door for her. The warmth of the night stole her breath. Stan led her over to a dark blue Chevy Tahoe. He opened the driver's door for her.

Nora turned toward him in amazement. "This is your second car? It's probably worth more than everything I own."

He shrugged. "It's just a car, Nora, nothing more. Just a possession."

"But it looks brand new. Are you sure you want to loan it to me?"

"Absolutely. Your girls will be safe when you drive. Here are the keys."

His hand touched her elbow as she climbed in. It raised her pulse. The new car smell filled her lungs as she checked out the interior. Stan entered and smiled.

"Uh, this car is beautiful, but you lied to me."

He laughed. "What? Why would you say that?"

"This car only has eight hundred miles on it!"

"Yeah, okay. Why would you say I lied?"

"It's practically brand new."

Stan laughed. "I did tell you I have a Vette, right?" Nora nodded. "So when I moved here, I just needed a second vehicle to drive in bad weather. I got a great deal on this. It was a demonstrator. Is there a problem with the Tahoe? Would you rather have the Corvette?"

Her joke hadn't gone as she intended. "No, I don't mean to be ungrateful, Stan. This is just, I can't find the right word... extremely generous, I guess."

Stan again touched her, which sent a tingling sensation up her arm. "Nora, we're friends. Friends do things for each other all the time. Just to make it clear, I'm not doing this to show off. I'm doing this because you are my friend and I care about you. There are more important things than money in this world."

In the glow of the dome light, Stan's sincerity could easily be seen.

Nora took a deep breath to prevent her voice from cracking, "Th-thank you. This is the nicest thing anyone has done for me or the girls in a long, long time."

Stan smiled, but Nora thought she could see sadness in his eyes. She looked away. *This is pathetic.* Someone loaning a clean car was the nicest thing anyone had done for her? It was more than her fiancé had done anyway. When she told Tim things were tough, he just told her to tighten her belt and dig in.

She was glad Stan came back. She had room in her life for a close friend.

Stan cleared his throat. "Are you all right?"

She refocused. "Sure. Why?"

"I was just wondering if you were going to start the car," he laughed.

She gave him a little smirk before reaching over to punch his arm. "Smarty! Did you have time to fix my car yet? I mean, I don't want to impose upon you."

Stan threw his hands up in the air. "Typical woman! Try to do something nice and you have to rub it in my face that I failed to get something else done!"

His comment struck a nerve. Her eyes stung. "Stan, I'm sorry. I was trying to joke with you. I didn't mean..."

He patted her hand, backing it up with a smile. "Hey, I was trying to joke with you, too. Don't read anything into it."

"Okay," she said sadly, "sorry about that. I need to pick up the girls. By the way, why'd you drop your Vette at my apartment? I could have driven you home."

He continued to smile at her, his eyes twinkling in the dome light. "I wanted to get the keys to your car so I can work on it tomorrow."

"Oh, I see." She was hoping it had been for another reason.

Stan looked away. "We should probably get going."

They drove to Nora's sitter. Upon arriving, she turned to him. "I'll be back in a little bit. It's always the same. Cassie and Tina will both be sound asleep. I'll end up carrying them out, so it will take me a few minutes. I hope you don't mind waiting."

He touched her arm. "I don't mind, but maybe you'd like some help? I'd be glad to."

She bit her lip. "That would be an imposition..."

His smile returned. "Nora, let's get something straight. Friends do things because they want to. If there is something I don't want to do, I'll tell you. But I can't see a time in my life when you would be an imposition. Tell you what. I'm coming in with you, unless you object."

She just stared at him for a long moment. Was there something he was trying to tell her? She couldn't read his mind, but the wheels started turning.

She could feel a smile fill her face. "Thank you. That would be nice."

As Nora predicted, both her girls were sound asleep and had no desire to wake up. Stan carried her older daughter Cassandra while Nora carried Martina. When they reached Nora's apartment, Stan picked up Cassandra again.

"Do you mind waiting while I tuck in the girls?" Nora asked.

"Sure. I can wait."

Just before Nora returned to where Stan waited, she thought she heard the kitchen cupboard door close. Stan was looking around her apartment. *I can imagine how it looks.* The furniture is clean, but old. The morning dishes were stacked in the sink, waiting to be washed. Laundry was washed and dried but still waiting on the small table to be folded. What did Stan's apartment look like? Or even more, she wondered, what did the home he shared with his wife look like? Did she keep it neat? *Why did she stay in California if he works here?*

***

Stan had stolen a quick look in the cabinets and fridge. Mother Hubbard's cupboard was almost completely bare. Sadness filled his heart for Nora. It seemed her life was so hard. It wasn't fair for someone so special to have to suffer like this.

Nora stooped to pick up something from the floor. *Where the hell was her fiancé in all this?* If Nora was his... *She has a ring on her finger, you idiot.*

Maybe life would get better for her after she married in the spring. But it still nagged at Stan. Why wasn't the man she was in love with helping her out? Stan knew if she was his, he would stop at nothing to help her.

Her voice brought him back. "I know it's late, but would you like a cup of coffee?"

There was nothing Stan wanted more than to sit and talk with Nora, but he had a 6:00 A.M. meeting. There was also work that he had brought home which hadn't left his briefcase, but still needed attention. "I really can't. I have to go to work early. Tell you what. I'll stop by tomorrow night and see if I can figure out what's wrong with your car. Which one is it, by the way?"

She wrinkled her nose at him. "It's the rust speckled, puke green 1963 Chevy Impala four-door. The girls and I named it Hank."

"Hank?" Stan laughed. "Why did you name it Hank?"

She smiled sadly. "Do you know who Hank Williams senior is?"

"Of course I do."

"His songs are so sad and lonely. One of them is called 'Lost Highway'. That car reminds me of all I've lost." She pinched her lips together and turned away.

Stan came over and touched her shoulder. Nora grasped his hand tightly for a brief moment. When she released it an instant later, he quietly whispered, "Would you like to talk about it?"

She wiped her cheeks. "I'm sorry. I don't mean to keep you when you need to go."

He turned her head and looked into her eyes. "I'm still here and will be as long as you want me to be."

Nora searched his eyes, as if she was looking for something. "Are you sure you want to hear my sob story?"

He sat down on her worn little sofa and patted for her to sit next to him. "There's no place I'd rather be. Please tell me about it, but only if you want to."

She got a faraway look in her eyes. He noted an errant tear. "It wasn't always like this. Before Bob became ill, we had such a wonderful life. A beautiful house we turned into a home. A new car every other year. I took the girls shopping each weekend. Cassie and Tina both had beautiful rooms and lots of toys. My husband treated me like a queen, filling our home with flowers and love."

She stopped to take a deep breath. "And he would take us on such wonderful vacations. Just before he got sick, he took us to Disney World for a week. Life was perfect."

Stan just watched her eyes, thinking that she used to have everything he always wanted—a home, a family, children, love. Not for the last time, his heart filled with sadness for her.

"And then one day, Bob's headaches started. They weren't too bad, at first. He thought it was just from working so many hours. But they got worse, to the point where nothing seemed to help. We went to our family doctor, but he couldn't help. We saw doctor after doctor, to no avail."

Nora stopped to wipe her eyes. "They finally sent us to a neurologist who discovered an inoperable brain tumor. We tried every treatment they could find, but he slipped downhill. Each one was more and more expensive. The insurance covered some of it, but not everything. To pay the bills, I began selling things. First were the antiques Bob and I collected, followed by the furniture, his car and finally our home. I didn't care. I would have given everything to make him well. I would have given my life if his could have been saved. But instead, God took him from me, and from Cassie and Tina. Suddenly, he was gone, but the bills were still there. I owed almost ninety thousand dollars. My lawyer told me to file for bankruptcy, but I refused. Somehow, someway, I will find a way to pay back every cent I owe."

Her eyes met Stan's. They were wet.

"Sorry you asked?"

He brushed the hair from her face. "Not at all. I only wish I could help you."

"Just being here to listen is more than enough. Sure you don't want that cup of coffee?"

If only it weren't so late. "You have no idea how much I wish I could stay, but I really have to go. I'll take a look at Hank tomorrow. By the way, I might not make it to the diner. I have a conference call at seven tomorrow night. But I'll miss seeing you."

"Miss you, too. Want to come by on Friday?"

Stan frowned. "I want to, but can't. I have a retirement dinner for one of my chemists, but I'm looking forward to Saturday."

She looked disappointed when he bid her a good night.

Chapter 9

"I want to go next, Mama."

Nora smiled as Martina stood. Her daughter, the attorney. She began to pace in front of everyone as if she were making a closing argument.

"Dad was always my hero. I remember calling him Daddy even before you two got married. It's funny, I can't remember my own biological father, except for the stories Dad told me about him. He was so willing to keep the memory of my real father alive in me."

Martina stopped to study her fingernails. Her voice was an octave higher than normal. "My favorite memory of Dad is from when I was in college. I was having such a hard semester. In danger of failing my chemistry class, which would have ruined my dream of becoming an environmental lawyer."

Nora shook her head in amusement as Martina continued to pace.

"It was a Friday and I was dreading a long weekend of studying. But when I got back to the dorm, Daddy was waiting on me. He whisked me off to dinner and a movie."

Nora's heart swelled with pride. Pride for Martina, for Kelly, for all her girls.

"He spent the whole night bringing chemistry alive," Martina said. "He made it real. By Saturday morning, everything was crystal clear to me. I got an 'A' in chemistry that semester. We went out to breakfast and caught a nap in the afternoon. I slept in my bed and he slept on the floor. Saturday night, Daddy took me out to an elegant restaurant and spent all day Sunday with me."

Martina turned away, but Nora caught the quick wipe of her cheek. She turned swiftly. "We went shopping on Sunday. As he stood in the doorway to say goodbye, he looked me in the eye and told me how special I was and how proud he was of me. He said how much he loved me and how blessed he was to have me as his daughter. It was my favorite weekend of all time." She bit her lip and sat down.

You mean so much to every one of us. Come back, Stan.

***

After work on Thursday, Stan stopped by to check out Hank. He discovered that it wasn't the battery, but rather the voltage regulator. He picked up a new one Saturday morning. Arriving back at Nora's, he popped the hood. It didn't take him long to replace the faulty device. After starting old Hank, Stan did a quick check of the vehicle.

What a piece of crap. The valves tapped, the ball joints were shot, and the brakes were bad, to name the least. He also noticed that Hank was seven months out of inspection. When he fired up the motor, the pollution rolling out of the exhaust pipe would have shamed a Navy destroyer trying to lay down a smoke screen. The big stain under the motor made Stan wonder how any oil could possibly remain in the engine block. Stan shook his head. Not only was old Hank absolutely worthless, it was unsafe. He chewed on his cheek as he contemplated how to tell Nora.

As he stood there looking at the puke green Impala, a young voice called out to him, "Hey mister! What are you doing with our car? Better get away from it or I'll tell my mother on you!"

He turned around to see both of Nora's girls looking at him through the window screen. He waved, smiling, "Good morning, Cassandra! Good morning, Martina! How are you fine young ladies doing today?"

The older one replied, "How do you know our names?"

"I met you the other day. Don't you remember?"

Even through the window screen, he could see Cassandra wrinkle up her nose. "No. How do you know us? And whatcha doing with our car?"

"I know you because I am a friend of your mom. And as far as Hank, I was trying to get him running again."

"Please don't fix him."

Stan laughed. "Why not?"

Little Martina joined in. "Hank smells funny!"

Cassandra added, "We like Mommy's new car. The radio even works!"

Stan laughed so hard, he doubled over. As he leaned over, both girls started yelling, "Mommy! Mommy! Mommy's home!" Stan turned around to see the Tahoe pull up.

Nora waved at him, smiling ear to ear. *Wow. You're beautiful when you smile.*

She stepped out and waved at her girls. "Mommy will be up in a minute." Turning to Stan, she said, "So, did you get Hank fixed? If you did, I'll really miss driving your Tahoe. It's a very nice car."

Stan smiled at her. "So you really like driving it, huh?"

"Yep. That's one sweet ride. So, how is Hank?"

Stan crossed himself as if he were Catholic. "I think he's ready to be towed off into the sunset."

Fear filled her face. "What? What do you mean?"

Stan looked sadly at her. "I'm afraid it doesn't make any sense to dump money into Hank. Did you realize the inspection ran out last March?"

Nora shook her head.

"The engine has a severe oil leak and the ball joints are shot. The master cylinder has a crack in it and the brakes need to be replaced. I also found the power steering reservoir is almost rusted through, not to mention the leak in the radiator or the bad valve tap and the bald tires. Nora, I'm really concerned. I don't want you driving Hank because it's not safe for you or the girls."

She drew a deep breath. "I can't afford to buy another car. How much would it cost to fix this one?"

Stan started to calculate in his head. "I could do the repairs for free, but just parts alone would run eight or nine hundred dollars."

Her face lost all color. "Eight or nine hundred dollars! I can't even afford to spend fifty."

Stan felt so bad that he was the one to have to tell her the bad news. "I could loan you the money, but if you were going to spend that much, it should be on a different vehicle. How long ago did you buy it?"

"About a year ago. I had a nice station wagon, but I had to sell it to buy school clothes for the girls. I paid five hundred dollars for Hank." She wiped her eyes. "I got ripped off, didn't I?"

"I'm afraid so. But there is good news about your car." Stan smiled at her.

She looked at him quizzically. "What possible good news could come out of what you just told me?"

He gave her a wholesome smile. "You don't have to make a decision today. You still have the Tahoe to drive.

There is a possibility I could be wrong, so we could take it to a garage and ask for an estimate."

She shook her head. "Stan, I'm not going to continue to use your car. It will start snowing here in a couple of weeks."

He started to say something but she cut him off. "Friend or no friend, your other car is a Corvette and I won't let you drive that when you have a perfectly good car that's better in the snow. I don't care if I have to walk everywhere, that won't happen!"

Stan frowned and commented, "We'll see. Let's talk about it later."

"There is no talking about it. Did you get Hank running?"

"Yes. It was the voltage regulator."

She opened her purse and pulled out her tip money. "How much was it?"

"It was exactly one bowl of soup, a cup of coffee and half a sandwich."

"No, I want to pay for it."

He put on his best hurt face. "Do you consider me to be your friend?"

"Of course I do, Stan."

"You said the other day that you didn't have any friends. Is that still true?"

"Unfortunately, yes it is."

"So, if I follow the logical path and if I am your only friend, I must be your *best* friend."

She nodded, frowning at him. "I guess you are."

"Would you please say it?"

"Say what?"

"Would you please say, 'Stan, you are my best friend'?"

She rolled her eyes. "What is this about?"

"Please, just humor me. Please tell me I'm your best friend."

73

She sighed. "Stanley Jenkins, you're my best friend."

"And Nora Marie Crittendale, you're my best friend. And I want to thank you."

"Thank me? For what?"

"For saying that. I have not had a true best friend since high school. You made my day." She smiled. Well, just a little. "And that little smile you just gave me pays the bill, in full. Boy, am I hungry. Can we go inside now? Your girls were talking to me out of the window, but I'd like to meet them in person."

She looked at him strangely. "May I ask you a question, Stan?"

"Absolutely. Ask away!"

"You're married, right? So what are you doing here?"

"I am being a friend to you."

"Is that all?"

"Of course."

"Don't expect anything more out of this than friendship. If you do, you're barking up the wrong tree because I'm engaged to Tim."

"And I am married to Linda. Look, Nora, all I want to be is your friend. Living eighteen hundred miles away from Southern California is lonely. I'm not looking for romance, only friendship."

He shook his head. He thought he could read her mind.

"Nora, I can see this is troubling you. Tell you what, I'll just leave. Use the Tahoe for as long as you need. When you're done, simply return it. My address is on the owner's card. Sorry, Nora. I didn't mean to bother you."

Stan turned, gathered his tools and walked to the Vette. He was glad he wasn't facing her, because his eyes were getting scratchy. He opened the door, threw his tools behind the seat and started to get in.

"Stan, wait, please wait!"

He turned toward her. "Yes, ma'am?"

"Don't call me ma'am! Stan, I'm sorry. I was afraid you were just being nice to get something I am not willing to give."

"That was the farthest thing from my mind. I was only trying to be kind to an old friend. I'm sorry, Nora. I'm leaving now."

She put her hands on her hips. A frown covered her face. "You will not leave. I'll have you know I pay my bills and I owe you a meal. Don't make your best friend feel bad because you wouldn't let her pay her debts."

"All right," Stan sighed. "But as soon as the meal's over, I'll leave."

A slight smile turned the corners of her lips. "We'll see. Let's talk about it later. Why don't you come in and I'll make us some lunch?" She turned and walked toward the apartment building.

He hadn't moved when she reached the entrance.

Her smile was gone. She called, "Stan, please come in. I don't want to beg. I may not have much but I do still have my pride, you know. Don't make me beg my one and only friend to come in for a visit."

Stan nodded, stood up, locked his Corvette and walked toward her.

As soon as Nora opened the door, her girls flew into her arms. They clung to her, smothering her with hugs. Stan stood silently behind, observing the closeness of the family.

Suddenly little Cassandra noticed him and pointed at Stan. "Mommy, why's he here? He's a bad man!"

Nora turned to look at Stan.

She called me a bad man?

Nora's face was full of concern. There was no smile on her lips as she stared at him. She asked her daughter, "Why did you call him a bad man?"

"Because he tried to fix Hank! I don't want him to fix Hank. I like our new car."

Stan breathed a sigh of relief and Nora's expression calmed. She turned to Cassie, "He's just trying to help us. So girls, this is Stanley Jenkins." Turning to Stan, she introduced her young ladies. "This is Cassandra."

Cassandra curtsied. "Nice to meet you, Mr. Jenkins."

Stan extended his hand and bowed. "It is my pleasure to meet you when you are awake, Miss Crittendale. But would you please call me Stan and not Stanley or Mr. Jenkins?"

Cassie smiled. "And you may call me Cassie, not Cassandra or Elizabeth."

"Elizabeth? Why would I call you Elizabeth?"

"It's my middle name. What's yours?"

"My middle name? Arnold."

She let out a belly laugh. "That's a funny name."

Nora countered, "Let's not be rude, Cassandra Elizabeth."

Through her laughter, she apologized, "I'm sorry, Stan."

He smiled. "That's okay, Cassie. I think it's a funny name, too!" He turned to Martina. Her brown hair was naturally curly. She just stared at him with those big brown eyes. His heart started to melt. "And what should I call you, young lady?"

"Mawtina."

"Tina," Nora sighed, "please say it correctly and tell Mr. Jenkins your middle name."

Her face turned in anger. "Why can Cassie call him Stan but I have to call him Mister Jenkins?"

It was Stan's turn to laugh. "That's an excellent question. Please call me Stan."

Her pout turned into a smile. "Awright, Stan. My name's Martina Anne." He noted she said her name perfectly that time. "Wanna play Barbies with me?" She held up an old worn Barbie doll.

"Well, unless Mommy needs help in the kitchen, I'd be delighted!"

Nora smiled. "Go ahead. I'll fix lunch."

Stan got down on all fours to play with both girls. Out of the corner of his eye, he saw Nora observing. Stan made up an improvised story as they played together. The girls were great. *Exactly as I pictured a family.* Well, with one exception. This wasn't his family. He could tell by the laughter that the girls were having as much fun as he was.

"Time to eat," Nora called.

Stan chased the girls around the living room one last time before leading them to the sink to wash their hands. Martina was too short, so he picked her up.

"Where would you like me to sit?" he asked Nora.

"At the head of the table, naturally." Her eyes widened momentarily before she looked away.

Nora sat at the other end of the table so they were facing each other.

Stan looked at the girls and asked, "So who's going to say grace?"

Cassie asked, "What's that?"

"You know, saying a prayer of thanks for the meal."

Martina replied, "We say prayers before we go to sleep."

Stan looked at Nora. She turned her eyes away. *Great. She probably thinks I'm judging her.* He shifted his gaze to her girls. "That's great. Prayers are important." He looked at Nora with pleading eyes. "Would you mind or be offended if I said grace?"

Her face was turning red. "No. Please do."

Stan clasped his hands. The girls imitated his move.

"Heavenly Father, we thank you for the food we are about to receive. We ask you to bless it and also bless the maker of this food. And Lord, I would be wrong not to ask a special blessing on these three young ladies that I am eating with today. Amen."

While Nora didn't have much to say, her daughters did. They told him all about their schools, their toys and the TV shows they liked. They both raved about the Muppets. Cassie told him how much she loved to go to the park and swing, but they didn't do that anymore.

"If you like to swing so much, Cassie, why don't you do it more often?"

"There are bad men there."

Stan looked at Nora with a question in his eyes.

Nora explained, "We went to the park about two weeks ago and there were several men there who said some very unsavory words to me in front of the girls. I felt it would be better if we avoided them, but I know the girls miss going to the park. We noticed those men there before and they always watched us, but this was the first time they said anything."

"What did they say?"

She shook her head. "I don't want to repeat it in front of the girls."

Cassie piped up, "They wanted Mommy to take off her clothes and dance with them."

"Cassandra! Be quiet."

Stan studied the three of them. "I'm sorry to hear that." He had to breathe deeply to dissipate the anger. Turning to the girls he said, "Just so you know, ladies, real men never talk to women like that. I'm sorry you had to hear that."

The girls continued to tell Stan all about their lives. Nora remained quiet.

When they finished eating, Stan said, "That was a wonderful meal, but the company was the best part."

"It was nothing. Don't make something out of nothing."

Stan turned to the girls and bowed. "And ladies, I'm honored to have dined with you!" They both giggled. "Why don't the two of you play while I help Mommy do the dishes?"

Nora shook her head. "You don't have to do that, Stan."

"Nonsense. I want to." He stood up and quickly cleared the table. As he ran the dishwater, he asked, "Would you like to wash or dry?"

"You don't have to do this."

He gave her a cross look, followed by his best smile. He kept smiling until she gave in.

"Oh, all right. Why don't you wash? I'll dry and put the dishes away."

Stan not only washed the lunch dishes, but also did the breakfast dishes. The girls were playing with their Barbies, using the same storyline Stan had made up for them. He quietly asked, "What happened at the park?"

Nora frowned. "I think those men were high. They were saying awful things about me, in front of the girls. They said they wanted me to take off my clothes and do nasty things with them. It was horrible! I grabbed the girls and started walking home. But they followed us and then their conversation became much viler. They told me they wanted to party with me."

Anger clouded his face. "What happened?"

"A police car drove past and slowed down. Luckily they turned away."

Stan ran his hand through his hair. "Would you like me to get involved?"

"No, please don't. We just won't go back there again, that's all."

"You and your girls have the right to go to a park and not be accosted. Is there another park nearby?"

"The closest one's about ten miles away. I didn't like to drive Hank that far."

"You have the Tahoe, now. Hey, what would you think if the four of us went there today?"

"That would be an imposition, Stan."

He was concentrating on scrubbing the morning's frying pan. "No, actually it wouldn't be. Please? I'd love that. Excellent practice for someday when I have girls of my own. And besides, I think your princesses might enjoy it." She didn't answer right away, so he looked at her. Her face was smiling and she nodded.

They packed up the girls in the Tahoe and headed toward the distant park. On the way, they passed the local one and Cassie said, "Look Mommy, it's those bad men." She pointed out the window.

Nora floored the engine, spinning the tires as she quickly drove away. "Cassandra, how many times have I told you... it's rude to point. Don't do that anymore!"

Stan hadn't done anything other than look out the window, but their faces were emblazoned in his mind. He would never forget.

They arrived at the park twenty minutes later. For a while, Stan and Nora walked around a short path while the girls played together. "You told me you're engaged," Stan said. "What was his name? Tim?"

"Yes. He's on the road a lot. A large sales territory. He's coming into town Friday night. Want to meet him?"

Afraid I might have something nasty to say to him. "I can't this weekend. I'm heading out to L.A. on Wednesday afternoon and will be there for a week."

Her silence caught his attention. When he turned toward her, she quickly turned away. He didn't recognize the look on her face.

"So you'll get to see Linda. Bet you're looking forward to that."

Right. Stan looked away. "Yeah, it'll be good to be back home. Nothing like the hustle and bustle of Los Angeles."

It seemed to Stan they both had more they wanted to say, but Martina came over, grabbing Nora's hand. "Mommy, Mommy, please push me!"

Nora rolled her eyes. "Sure, sweetheart."

Cassandra also ran over and grabbed Stan's hand, begging, "Push me, Stan, push me!"

Nora looked at her daughter sternly. "Cassie, where are your manners? Did you say please?"

"Please push me on the swings, Stan!"

"Of course. Let's race Mommy and Tina," he said.

Cassandra nodded and took off. Nora grabbed Martina, following suit.

Stan laughed and ran slower. At the swings, Nora and Stan took turns pushing the girls. They sang silly songs and told funny stories which her daughters absolutely loved. They decided to call it a day about an hour before sunset. When they got to the Tahoe, Stan asked Nora if she would mind if he drove.

They headed back in the general direction of Nora's apartment, but near the midway point, Stan turned left.

Nora asked, "Where are we going?"

"I don't know about you girls, but I'm in the mood for pizza. Anyone else?"

Before Nora could respond, her girls yelled in unison, "Yeah!"

They ate at a local pizza parlor before stopping at a drive-in for dessert. It was close to the girl's bath time when Stan walked the three ladies back to their apartment.

Both girls gave Stan a hug before heading to the room they shared to get ready for their baths. Nora walked Stan to the door. "Thank you for a wonderful day. I appreciate everything you did for us. Will I see you this week?"

"I might stop at the restaurant on Tuesday. Did I tell you I'll be in L.A.?"

Nora studied a spot on the floor, answering slowly, "Yes, I remember. I have to tell you, I'll miss you. Hey, I have an idea! How about coming over tomorrow?"

Stan frowned. "I can't. I have plans, but could we do dinner on Monday?"

She smiled. "I'd like that, but please don't expect anything spectacular."

"I hope you realize it isn't the food I like, but the company. Goodnight, Nora." Stan headed for the door, but suddenly pivoted to look at her. "And just to let you know, I've got dinner. Just bring your appetite."

***

After tucking the girls in, Nora brewed a cup of tea. If she breathed deeply, she could still pick up his scent. *Stan.* Why did you come back into my life? *Just to be my friend?*

Listening to the girls and Stan play earlier made her realize how much she missed being part of a family, a complete family. She allowed her mind to drift. *What would it have been like if I'd married you?* Would we have been happy?

This sucks. It was fruitless. Nora drained her cup and placed it in the sink. She walked back to the bathroom. The reflection in the mirror was someone whose life hadn't turned out as she hoped. Losing her husband. Working long hours trying to make ends meet. Bringing her girls up by herself. Lowering her standard to marry a man she would never love, just because he would be a good provider.

She studied the wrinkles around her eyes. She knew what she wanted. *Why did you have to be married? Did you really come back into my life just to be my friend?*

Chapter 10

$\mathcal{N}$ora's heart was warmed by the memories her family shared. Kaitlin's voice was next.

"Daddy was always so sweet, especially to me."

Kelly laughed, feigning anger. "That's because you were his favorite—Daddy's little girl."

"Tsk, tsk," Nora said. "Stop it, Kelly. When one of you was suffering or sad or in trouble, that's when you were his favorite."

Kaitlin was biting her lower lip. "The summer between elementary school and middle school was tough for me. Cassie had Ellie. She and her husband moved to Savannah. Tina married Gary and moved away. Kelly was away at cheerleading camp. And Mom went to Europe with Grandma."

Nora remembered that summer well. And what Stan did.

"When Dad left for work on Monday morning, I was so lonely. Then a couple hours later, he came home. We packed and he took me away to New England, just the two of us. He made me feel so special. I remember walking down this road in Maine. He held my hand and told me that he raised four princesses, but I was his favorite."

Kelly pointed as she turned to Martina. "Um-huh. See, counsellor. The witness's testimony supports my supposition."

Martina snickered, "Inadmissible. She wasn't under oath."

Cassandra let out a belly laugh. "I object."

Martina turned to her. "On what grounds?"

"Daddy told me I was his favorite."

Kelly moaned, "Oh no, not another one. That's because you were the first born."

"Over-ruled," said Martina. "I was his favorite."

Geeter piped up. "Y'alls wrong."

Their heads turned in unison. His wife Kelly said, "What's that supposed to mean?"

Geeter pointed at Nora. "Ever see the way he looks at Mom? She's his favorite."

***

On Sunday afternoon, Stan drove past the park. He paused at a stop sign, glancing toward the playground. There they were, sitting at a picnic bench. He drove his Vette around the back of the large four-story apartment building that faced the park.

Stan removed a large Igloo lunch pail that carried something he had taken from work that morning and also something he'd purchased at the grocery store. He entered the apartment building from the back, walked down the hallway and exited from the front of the building. He arrived at the park, and sat at a table not far from the three 'bad men'.

Stan removed a can of Shasta soda and some Twinkies from the cooler. He observed the trio and noted a couple of things that really didn't surprise him. The first was the bottle in their brown bag. It was large, and he caught a whiff of whiskey when one of them let out a loud burp. The second thing he picked up on was the joint they were sharing.

As Stan sat eating his snack, they lit up and shared several more joints. *Think you own the park, don't you?*

The fat one pulled out a can of spray paint and painted a dirty picture on the side of a building. Looking around, Stan saw lots of graffiti on just about every surface. He knew who had painted it there.

They ignored him, instead focusing on the women who brought their children to the park. A pretty blonde, probably in her early thirties was on the see-saw with her daughter, a girl of maybe eight. The woman was wearing a short gray mini-skirt and black legwarmers.

The tall skinny punk wearing a torn Army coat started talking loudly to her. "Hey lady! Whatcha wearing under the mini-skirt? Give us a look-see!"

The second of the trio was a heavy set man, probably in his early twenties. He was wearing a filthy torn hooded jacket. "To hell with the look!" he yelled. "Drop the tall socks, lift your skirt up and bend over the table. I want to do you from behind!"

That was about all Stan could stomach. He started to get up when the third one, a very muscular man probably in his mid-twenties said viciously, "You two can have the mother. I want the girl." The muscular man got up and moved toward the woman and her daughter.

That did it! Stan quickly re-packed his food and got up, carrying the cooler with him. He glanced at the young woman, who was holding her daughter and now staring at the junkies with fear in her eyes. Stan sat the cooler down on a picnic table. The three were bullies. Stan learned long ago how to deal with those kind of people.

He yelled at them, "Hey! Didn't they teach you girls down in juvenile detention not to talk like that to women?"

The muscular one glanced at Stan dismissively and said, "Screw you, old man. Get lost."

"Anyone tell you that you lack manners? Maybe I need to teach you some."

The heavy set one turned away from the girl and moved toward Stan. "Hey, you old bastard, up your nose with a rubber hose! Now get out of here before I beat the crap out of you!"

Stan looked the muscular one up and down. "So are these two your girlfriends or are you the female in this relationship?"

By now all three of them had lost interest in the woman and her daughter. All their attention was focused on Stan. He thought they were thinking if the old dude wanted trouble, it would be three against one. They couldn't lose.

The heavyset man asked, "Who the hell are you, old man?"

"Just one of many. You aren't the only one who has a gang."

The skinny one scoffed. "Yeah? I don't see no one but you."

"That's because we only allow you to see us when we want you to."

The skinny one looked around like he was scared. *Good*, Stan thought. *Weed-induced paranoia. That'll work in my favor.*

Muscles stated, "If you got a gang, what's your gang's name?"

"Broad Street Park Vigilantes. So which one of you girls is the leader?"

Muscles looked pretty upset. "This is my gang! Call me a girl one more time and I'll kick your ass!"

Stan shrugged. "If you insist. You're a pathetic little girl!"

Muscles charged at him. Stan ducked the blow. The assailant tried to turn, but with such momentum, the back of his leg struck the picnic table bench, dropping him to a sitting position. Muscles' body slammed into the unforgiving wood of the table. The injured man screamed, "My back, my back." He writhed on the ground, crying like a little baby.

The fat one charged next. Stan side-stepped just in time. Mr. Obesity ran right into one of the bouncy horses on a large metal spring. Hands on his crotch, he moaned before falling over. The attacker was flat on his back.

Stan glanced at Muscles and that glance almost cost him the fight. The skinny one came in with a haymaker punch. Stan didn't even have time to evade. Luckily, the impaired man swung too soon. The action of not making the contact he'd anticipated resulted in an unbalanced charge. The skinny kid's head struck a tall oak tree with a dull thud. All three youths were down and Stan hadn't even thrown a punch.

Stan then walked over to Muscles. "So, you're the leader of this little Brownie troop, right?" Stan placed one foot on the thug's chest. "I guess I need to help you earn your manners badge. First off, you don't talk to women or children like that. Do you understand?" Muscles cursed at him. Stan took his other foot and started grinding his heel viciously into the punk's groin. The man screamed in pain. "Getting me yet?"

Stan stepped off and approached the heavy set one as he tried to get up. Stan pushed against his forehead. The big man fell backwards. The skinny one had made it to his knees. When Stan walked toward him, the boy lunged. Stan jumped out of the way, feeling the breeze as he barreled past. For the second time, the kid struck his head against an immovable object, this time a light pole. The punk crumpled. All of them were now writhing on the ground.

One by one, Stan grabbed them and seated all three at the picnic table. Standing in front of them, he lectured, "Okay girls, now you'll listen to me. We're going to have a short conversation, so I'll use small words. We have been watching you for a while." He pointed over his shoulder at the apartments. All three of them gave the building painful glances. "We've watched you idiots bully and terrorize women and children for way too long. It stops now. But today's your lucky day. I'll give you the chance to leave in just a moment. But first, I'm going to show you something and I want you to pay very, very close attention."

Stan placed the cooler on the table, opening it to remove a small Igloo thermos, two thick gloves and a large, long chunk of sausage. He donned the gloves, unscrewing the thermos lid. A steam-like vapor slowly curled above its top. "Pay close attention, girls. You'll need to watch this. See, this sausage looks like a certain body part you may or may not have, wouldn't you agree?" He waved the limp chunk of meat in the air. "I want you to know I have magical powers. Watch what happens when I stick it in this special thermos."

Stan did as he stated before removing the sausage. "Now notice what happens when I strike it against the bench." He slammed the now frozen hunk of meat against the top of the picnic table where it shattered into a million pieces. "Bad things happen when I get upset. Wouldn't you agree?"

Their mouths dropped open and three sets of eyes grew large with fear.

"I'm sure you are all pretty smart girls, well... relatively, so you can put together the imagery. And we know so much more about you than you think—like where you hang out, where you live and even which room you sleep in. You'll listen to exactly what I say and follow my instructions or the next time, it won't be a sausage that gets shattered, but instead it will be a body part that's very near and dear to you. With me?"

He stopped to study them. He had their attention.

"First, you'll leave this park when I tell you to. Second, you will return at exactly nine o'clock tonight and cover every inch of graffiti with a clean coat of paint. Third, when you're done, you'll leave this park forever and never, ever return. If any of us catch sight of you or hear that you ever spoke to a woman or a child the way I heard you talk today, we'll hunt you down. If we see you anywhere near this park ever again, we'll come for you and there'll be hell to pay. Now, is that perfectly clear?"

All three nodded their heads.

"Now get out of here before I decide to kick your asses just for spite!" Stan packed and picked up the Igloo, but the punks hadn't moved. He unzipped and removed the thermos again. "Still here? Who wants to go first?" Stan took a step toward Muscles, but all three got up and ran away.

The woman and her child were still standing nearby, just staring at him. Stan emptied the thermos onto the ground where it made a nice white cloud of smoke.

"Don't worry, the smoke's absolutely harmless. I don't think you will ever have to worry about them again. If they come back, I'll deal with them." He walked across the street, entered the apartment building, walked down the hall, exited and finally climbed into his Corvette. He smiled to himself as he drove away. *That one was for Nora.*

***

Nora rubbed her aching back. The Monday morning breakfast rush finished just after ten. The lunch crowd wouldn't start until eleven-thirty. Nora had refilled the condiments and napkins at all the tables in her station. She was picking up a morning paper someone had abandoned when she saw it. The front page headline read, "Vigilante Attacks Youths at Broad Street Park!" But it wasn't the headline that caught her eye. It was the police artist's sketch. The face looked vaguely familiar.

Her mouth went suddenly dry. There was a resemblance to Stan. She read the article closely. It said that a group of youths had been making loud and threatening comments to a woman and her daughter, when out of nowhere, this Vigilante appeared. He used martial arts skills to attack the youths. After viciously beating them, he then forced them to sit down and watch him perform a weird science experiment. The Vigilante had threatened the boys' lives, according to witnesses.

Nora guessed exactly who the boys were. When she read about the weird experiment, she realized it fit perfectly with Stan's chemistry background. Her high school teacher had performed a similar experiment using liquid nitrogen.

She knew Stan was the Vigilante. She went on to read that police had raided the park later in the evening, based on an anonymous tip. That raid resulted in the arrest of the same three youths for defacing community property as well as charges for drug possession with the intent to distribute. They would be going to jail for several years.

Nora put down the paper in disgust. Here, these boys were accosting innocent people *and* arrested for breaking the law, yet the paper was calling for the community to identify the Vigilante. Talk about yellow journalism! *What's wrong with this country?*

Yet knowing Stan was the Vigilante sent a shiver up her spine. He could end up in jail because of what he'd done. Still something else bothered her on a deeper level. If Stan was capable of that much reported violence, was he a danger to her and her girls? She and Stan were going to have a serious talk when he came over for dinner that night.

Stan arrived at six, carrying a crock pot, a bag of vegetables, and dinner rolls. She could smell the roast and peeked in to see the potatoes and carrots in the crock pot as well. Nora held her tongue while he dished out supper and also while they ate.

After dinner, Nora bathed her girls and got them ready for bed, while Stan sweetly did the dishes. He came back to say goodnight, but Nora asked him to stay. She told him she had something to talk to him about.

After she put the girls to bed, she sat across the table from Stan. "How was your day yesterday? What'd you do?"

He spoke, but his eyes failed to make contact with hers. "Oh, it was a pleasurable day. I watched the Lions tromp the Giants on television."

"Really? Do anything else?"

He had a suspicious look in his eyes. "Not really, why?"

"Read today's paper?"

"No, why do you ask?"

She walked to the kitchen, returning with the morning newspaper. She threw it down in front of him. "You might want to look at the front page. Take a good look. Maybe I'm wrong, but I think you're the person in that sketch."

Stan's face turned white. "I-I-I don't know what you mean. This guy, what did they call him, the Vigilante? He doesn't look anything like me."

"You sure?"

"Y-yes."

She slammed both hands on the table as her face turned red. "Dammit, Stan. I like you a lot, but let me tell you something. I will not tolerate a liar in my house or around my girls. You'll consider that if you value our friendship at all. Now, let me ask you one more time. What did you do yesterday, say around one o'clock?"

Stan looked her in the eye this time. "I'm sorry for lying to you. Yes, that was me."

"I *knew* it was you! After I asked you not to get involved, you went and attacked those boys? And I know you learned the hot dog trick from Mr. Albright, didn't you?"

"It was a hunk of sausage, not a hot dog."

"Okay, sausage then! Why'd you do this?"

He was quiet for a minute. "I did it because they had no right to say what they did to you. I went to observe them and they were doing the same thing to another woman. I believe they were going to attack her and it was too much for me. They deserved much more than what they got. I honestly believe they will never come back to that park again. It should be safe for you and the girls. I did it for the three of you, Nora."

Her anger started to boil over. "No. No they won't be back for say five to ten years. It seems someone tipped off the police they would be there last night. Would you happen to know anything about that?"

Stan nodded slowly.

"What, were they high?"

"I think so."

"And you beat them senseless?"

"Actually, no. They beat themselves. I didn't even have to strike a blow."

"That doesn't seem logical. Why should I believe you?"

His eyes were clear as he searched hers. "I'm telling you the truth. I did what I did because I believed it had to be done."

"Why am I not surprised? You do realize the police are actively looking for you, don't you? And they will arrest you if they find you. You could go to jail. Was it really worth it?" Her lips turned into a fine white line.

"If it means the three of you can go to the park without them mouthing off or attacking you," Stan murmured, "then the answer is yes."

She just stared at him for a moment before saying, "Don't you ever come to the restaurant again. Do you hear me?"

Stan sighed and shook his head. "So that's it, huh? I suppose you don't ever want to see me again? And I suppose this means our friendship is over?"

No! Nora gave him a confused look. "That's not what I'm saying at all. I just don't want you to come to the restaurant because police officers eat there all the time. If I recognized you, they will, too. I don't want you getting into trouble!"

The tenseness in his face dissipated. "I see. So what do you suggest?"

"I don't know. But if we go out together, it can't be at the restaurant. I would suggest you stay out of public places for a while."

One question still filled Nora's mind.

"While we're on this subject, may I ask something else?"

"Yes, of course."

"Are you really a martial arts master like the paper says?"

"I wouldn't believe everything you read in the paper."

She eyed him warily. "You told me you were a tank mechanic in the Army. Was that a lie, too?"

"No," Stan shook his head. "I was exactly what I told you, nothing more. But when I was in Europe, I had some friends in the 82nd Airborne. They taught me a few things."

Should I believe him? Her eyes searched his for the answer. Her mind quickly answered.

"May I ask another personal question... and will you be totally honest?" Despite trying to avoid it, she felt the corners of her lips curl.

"I learned my lesson. You can ask me absolutely anything and I'll be totally honest. I won't risk our friendship again."

As Nora observed him, she noted a strange look in his eyes. He was holding something back.

"What did you want to ask me, Nora?"

She looked back the hall at the room her daughters shared to make sure they weren't eavesdropping. "So tell me, what did it feel like when you slammed that hot dog against the picnic bench and it shattered into a million pieces?" A giggle escaped from her.

Stan looked shocked. His laughter joined hers. "It blew their drug-induced minds! I chased them off and as they ran away, I kept thinking just one thought..."

Nora laughed, nodding. "Go ahead."

"All I could think was something Mr. Albright used to say. Remember?"

"Mr. Albright?"

"Yep. He used to say... Better living through..."

It came back to her. She blurted out, "Better living through chemistry." Nora laughed so hard that she had to excuse herself as she ran to the bathroom.

They talked until very late. Since Stan couldn't come to the restaurant, they said goodbye. Nora asked him to come over Friday night for dinner instead. Stan quickly agreed. He gave her a quick hug and said goodnight. After he left, Nora stood with her back to the door for a few minutes, lost in thought. She cherished the hug and realized she missed him already.

Her mind drifted to Tim and the relationship they had. Even when he was gone for weeks at a time, she rarely missed him. But Stan. He was so easy to talk to. He always made her feel great. The girls loved him. He really cared for them and, she realized, he cared for her. But he was married. She hoped Linda appreciated what she had.

Wiping a tear from her eye, Nora headed off to bed.

***

Stan had an early morning flight, but before he drove to the airport, he made four stops. The first was to Nora's apartment complex to retrieve his Tahoe. The second was to a gas station to fill up the gas tank. The third stop was to a grocery store where he bought a few things for the girls. And finally, he drove back to Nora's apartment. He left the Tahoe with a full tank of gas, several bags of non-perishable food, a handwritten note and an envelope tucked in the console. He gazed at the apartment Nora shared with her daughters and said a little prayer asking God to watch over them.

He arrived in Los Angeles early enough to be at the headquarters by noon. The man who hired him, Joe Summers, passed him in the hallway. "Stanley Jenkins! Just the man I was thinking about. How have you been?"

"Great, Joe. How's life here in beautiful Southern California?"

"Hot, dry and sunny. Do you like Detroit? You used to live there, right?"

"It's okay. I lived there when I was a kid."

"So, it was like going back home again, right? Lots of good memories?"

"Actually, no. My childhood wasn't the best. It's not my favorite place in the world."

Joe patted him on the shoulder. "Sorry to hear that. And after the thing that happened between you and Linda, I'm so sorry."

Stan nodded and suddenly found himself fighting back sorrow. "Thanks, Joe."

"Ever been to Chicago, Stan?"

Chicago? "I was there once on a bus trip in high school, why?"

"You like it?"

"Yeah, but why are you bringing up Chicago?"

"Because," he paused for effect, "we're in the process of buying out another large polymer company. Their main research and development lab is there—a state of the art lab. There's where we'll develop all of our new products. It's our future. And we need someone very bright and intelligent to manage it, to guide our future." Joe studied Stan's reaction.

"Really?"

"Know what? I think you're the one to run it. We need someone to guide the direction and dream the visions of our future. I think that's also you. I told the board the same thing... that is, I think you're our man. I know you have meetings and training this week, but stop by my office say, Thursday afternoon. I'd like to discuss the possibility with you. Interested?"

Stan was floored! This was a total surprise. "Uh, why me? You have more senior managers in the company who would be better qualified."

"Maybe, but you impressed quite a few people with all those patents and new products you developed when you were here. Just think about it a little before you stop by. If it's not something you want, that's okay." He looked at his watch. "Stan, I've got to go. Another meeting, you know. They never seem to end. See you Thursday!" Joe shook Stan's hand and walked off to his meeting.

Stan stood there flabbergasted. This was way too good to be true! He hated to wish his life away, but he could barely wait for Thursday afternoon.

On Wednesday evening, he stopped by Ricardo's. He loved the restaurant, but going there was bittersweet. He and Linda had often frequented Ricardo's. They seated him near the door. He ordered chicken marsala.

He recognized one of the patrons—a young pop singer who was in high demand. As he sat staring at her, a familiar voice said, "Hello, Stan. Never thought I'd see you again, especially in L.A."

Stan turned quickly and found himself staring at his soon to be ex-wife Linda and a man who was quite a bit older than her, although he was well tanned and in shape. Stan stood up and greeted them both. "Never thought I'd see you again, either. How've you been?"

She looked radiant. "Very well, thank you. I'd like to introduce you to Albert. Stan, this is Albert. Albert, Stan." They shook hands and the older man gripped Stan's hand tightly as if to emphasize his strength.

To Stan's immense relief, his waitress delivered his order. Linda said goodbye and excused the two of them. Stan had lost his appetite, but mechanically chewed his meal and made a quick retreat. He'd never come back to Ricardo's again. As he stood at the door to leave, he shook the dirt off his feet, just like Jesus had told His followers to do when they left an unfriendly town. This was no longer his restaurant... or his town.

Seeing Linda bothered him very much. He thought of how much he had loved her, how his hopes and dreams had hung on their relationship. And now it was gone. He was just an old acquaintance to her. He drove around in his rental car, feeling lonely. He wished he had a friend, someone he could talk to. When he arrived back at his hotel, he decided to call Nora. It was just after eight-thirty in L.A., so her children would probably be in bed. He hoped she wasn't.

***

Nora was just finishing up the dishes when the phone rang. By the time she dried her hands, the phone was on its ninth ring. She quickly picked it up. "Hello?"

Her chest warmed when she heard his voice. "Hi, Nora. It's Stan. Is it too late?"

She sensed something was wrong. "No, is everything okay?"

He hesitated. "I just needed someone to talk to. I got some wonderful news today I wanted to share. Sure this isn't a bad time?"

Wonderful news, and you picked me to tell? "Actually, I was just thinking of you."

"Really? What were you thinking?"

How much I miss you. "I was thinking it was so kind of you to fill the gas tank. Oh, I don't know if you realized it or not, but you left your groceries in the back seat."

"Uh, they weren't for me, but for the three of you. Did you look in the bags?"

Had he known how much they needed them? Her voice was a little higher when she responded, "You really shouldn't have, but thank you. No, I didn't look in the bags." Okay, that was a lie. "Why'd you do that?"

She picked up the humor in his voice. "Guess I should let you in on a little secret. Are you sitting down?"

Her body started to tingle. *Tell me what I want to hear.* What was he going to say? "I am now. What's your secret?"

He stuttered a little. "M-my s-s-secret is, is that I've grown quite fond of a very close friend and those two beautiful daughters of hers. I love doing nice things for them."

Her voice was now playful. "You have, have you?" Was he trying to say something more? Her hands were trembling. "And just how fond are you of these three ladies?"

He paused and Nora knew he was looking for the right words. Was he trying to tell her his inner thoughts?

"Quite, quite fond. Please take the groceries. No offense, but I know times are tough on you and I just wanted to help out. I did it because I care, a lot."

How much? "Is, is that why you left me a little handwritten note?"

He laughed. Her mind went back to their talks years ago, when they were carefree and the world was full of promise.

"I wanted to brighten up your day and week. I know we're just friends, but I really miss being with you."

She was silent for a minute or two. "I really miss being with you, too." She had to control her emotions. She changed the subject. "You know the girls will be so jealous when I tell them you called. They both keep asking when you're coming over again."

They talked until well after midnight. Stan asked about her day and Nora told him how rough it had been. She still hadn't found a sitter to watch the girls at night, so she had to work the day shift. The problem with working days at the restaurant was that her tips were only about twenty-five percent of what she made when she worked nights. At this rate, she wouldn't be able to pay her rent or buy food for the girls.

Stan grew silent. "There's an envelope in the console of the Tahoe with five hundred dollars inside. Use the money in there if you need it."

Nora's eyes grew blurry at the generosity of his offer. "I don't want charity, Stan. I can't..."

"This isn't charity. Consider it a loan. Someday, you can pay it back, but only if you want to. You're my friend. Friends help each other and I want to help you."

"But I..."

"But nothing. I admire you for doing such a great job bringing up your girls as a single mother. Let me help make it easier."

"How would I ever be able to pay you back? I don't make enough when I work days."

"Then how about if I babysit the girls, say one or two evenings a week, just until things get better."

The girls would love it. "That's so generous, but I don't know."

Stan hesitated in his response. "If you don't feel comfortable with me watching the girls..."

"No, no. It's not that at all. It's just, well, it's such a big imposition. Giving up your evenings to watch them."

His response was very quick. "I don't mind. Why don't you think about it?"

Her voice was breathless. She knew what she wanted to say. "Sure you wouldn't mind?"

"Not at all, but you think about it and let me know."

"Okay, I will. So how was your day?"

"I've got something to tell you." The excitement in his voice raised her hopes.

Could it be? "What's that?"

"Chicago." Over the next five minutes, he filled her in. The responsibilities would be immense, but it was what he loved and wanted to do. He told her he'd already made up his mind that if offered, he'd take it.

She was happy for him, but the sadness inside her grew like a weed. "When will this happen?"

"I don't know. Acquisitions can take a long time. It might be months or years until it happens. Besides, you'll be married long before then."

Thanks for reminding me.

A long silence followed. "You okay, Nora?"

"Yes, yes. Sorry. Look, I need to get going."

"Uh, okay. Can I call you tomorrow? I'll know more about it then."

"Yes. I'd like that." They set up a time after the girls went to bed.

Nora stared at the wall, missing him so much.

***

Seventeen hundred miles west, Stan opened the sliding glass door. He stepped into the warm night air, listening to the cacophony of traffic noise. But he didn't really hear it. All he heard was the silence in Nora's voice when he made the comment about her getting married. Something wasn't right about that whole relationship.

He tried to look for stars, but the light pollution kept them at bay. She was engaged to Mr. Wonderful, but he seemed to be non-existent. Was the fiancé even real?

If you were mine, Nora, I'd shower you with love so...

He shook his head and muttered, "Get real, Jenkins. She's not yours and never will be. Quit torturing yourself."

He re-entered the room, pulling the curtain closed. The air conditioning felt good. He turned on a western, enjoying the simplicity of the show. *Life was so much simpler... back then.* He watched the TV, but the only thing he really saw was Nora's face.

***

Nora sat by the phone that Thursday night. As she waited, she contemplated their relationship. Just like high school, the thought of Stan turned her on immensely. She remembered the taste of his kisses, the closeness and camaraderie that had developed so quickly. She also remembered when she had made the decision to break her engagement with Bob to be with Stan. But then Stan completely disappeared from her life, so she never went through with breaking off the engagement. Bob slowly filled the void that Stan's departure had left. In time, she fell deeply in love with Bob.

Then there was her current fiancé. Her relationship with Tim was even less appealing than the beginning had been with Bob. Tim was a safety relief for her. He'd give her daughters a good home. As far as love, well, that didn't even play into it. She'd agreed to marry him solely for her daughters' benefit.

The feelings she had for Stan were so much more, so strong. Was it love? Even after such a short period of time, she knew it was. They'd spoken more deeply, talked so much more in the short period since his return than Tim had in the entire time she had known him.

But Tim would be a good provider for her girls, she told herself. Yes, he had his flaws and the biggest one was that he was so self-centered. He loved to talk about himself. Stan was the complete opposite. He asked her what her opinion was, seemingly hanging on her every word.

There was only one problem. Stan was married. He already had a wife. Nora contemplated telling him how she truly felt. She sadly realized he was her soulmate. More than that, he was the greatest love of her life. Even though he had come into her restaurant just a few short weeks ago, she knew he was the man she needed, the one she wanted for life. And if she told him how she felt, what would happen? He rarely talked about Linda. She worried they didn't have a very good relationship, but could she stand looking at her reflection in the mirror if she broke them up? *No, I couldn't live with myself if I did.*

There were butterflies in her stomach when the phone rang. It killed her not to answer immediately and tell him she loved him. She waited until the fifth ring before picking up, "Hello?"

But the voice on the line wasn't Stan's. It was Tim's. "Hey, Nora. How's it been?"

"Uh, g-g-good. How are you?"

"That's what I'm calling about. My work plans changed and I won't be able to see you 'til Christmas Day."

"What? Why not?"

"Because they know I'm their best man. I'm what keeps the company afloat. And how do you reward the best? You send them across the pond. I'm going to Europe—France, Germany, Austria."

Nora heard a woman's voice call Tim's name. "Where are you? At the office?"

Hushed conversation on the other end of the line. "No, I mean yeah. At the office. Look. I won't be able to call for a while. The price on those trans-Atlantic phone calls won't be covered on my expense report and the way they rip you off on fees... Too danged expensive for my blood. Enough about me. How's it going?"

Nora's head was spinning. "My car died. The sitter cut back on watching the girls at night, so I have to work day shift. That makes everything tight financially. I'm not sure..."

He cut her off. "That's nice. I gotta get going. Just try a little harder to look for a night babysitter or get a better paying job. It's only for a couple of months, until we get married in April. Just hang in there. I can't wait to see the Eiffel Tower and..." Tim droned on for a few more sentences before saying goodbye. The entire conversation lasted maybe four minutes.

She had just returned the receiver to the cradle when it rang again. Thinking it might be Tim, she picked it up immediately. This time it was Stan. "Hi, Nora! How was your day?" She knew he was probably about to burst at the seams to tell her about his conversation regarding Chicago, but first, he talked to her for almost an hour about her day. He asked about the girls, if the Tahoe was running all right, whether she needed anything and about how she felt.

When she was talked out, he told her about the entire day before. "Nora, I found out more about Chicago. Want to hear about it?"

"Yes, please tell me."

"The plan is for the sale to be finalized on May first. If I get this position, I'll start my new job the next day. I'm so excited! I'll be in charge of research and development for the entire company! The future of my company—new products, growth and innovation—will be the responsibility of my group. Of course, it isn't set in stone yet. I have to meet with and be approved by the board. That will be the first week in December. If they approve, I'll be promoted to vice-president and not only that, I'll become a voting member on the board."

Nora was astounded. "Stan, I'm so proud of you! So glad and happy," she said, but the tone in her voice gave her away. She knew Stan heard something else.

"Nora, something wrong? Did I say something that bothered you?"

What's wrong with me? She was sad when she should be happy for him. "No Stan, it's nothing, really nothing. I'm very happy your dreams are coming true."

He was silent for a moment before replying, "You know, Nora, I won't put up with a friend who doesn't tell the truth. I know you, very well, maybe better than anyone else. Would you agree?"

The quickness of her response somehow surprised herself. "Yes, Stan. You know me better than anyone ever did or ever will."

"Then what's wrong? Please tell me."

"It's nothing, really."

"Nora, you know you're my best friend. You can tell me anything. Please share what's going through that pretty little head of yours."

You compliment me when what I really want is what I can't have. Why did he have to be married? She didn't respond for over a minute. "Stan, if you're really my best friend and you know me so well, why don't you tell me what I am thinking." In her heart of hearts, she prayed he would know what she wasn't able to say out loud.

Stan hesitated for a few seconds before responding, "I think you're happy for me, but sad because when I move to Chicago and you get married, you're afraid our friendship will diminish."

Tears stung her eyes. He knew part of her exact thoughts—except the part where he swept her off her feet and they lived happily ever after. "You got it, Stan. You hit the nail on the head. I finally found you again and I can't contemplate what my life will be like without you in it."

He whispered, "Oh, Nora."

Her mind took off like an out of control rocket. Why did he have to be married? Couldn't he see how much she cared? This was going to end up like the last time, when Nora wanted him but he disappeared on her. And this time? She wanted him, but knew it couldn't be. She would be stuck with someone else when she really wanted Stan.

Nora's chest tightened. If he was really her best friend, he should pick up on her feelings. But even if he did, he wouldn't be able to tell her. He was married. Her hopes and dreams would never come true.

Stan's voice snapped her back to reality. His whispered voice sent a shiver up her spine instead of calming her. "We'll find a way, my friend. We'll make a way. I promise you that, Nora. You are too important to me to just let our friendship wither."

This was too hard on her. She was about to lose it. She needed to hang up and now. "I've got to go, Stan. Martina is calling for me," she lied. "Can we talk again on

Monday night? I don't want to interfere with your weekend with Laura."

"Who?" he asked. "Oh. My uh... my wife's name is Linda. She's uh... out of town until Saturday morning. Can we talk tomorrow?"

This was killing Nora. She needed time to get her feelings under control. "No, I think Monday would be better." Something Stan had said suddenly nagged at her. "Say, you told me you're staying in a hotel. Why aren't you staying at home?"

His response was delayed. "Oh... because of the conference. Everyone has to stay at the hotel."

That sounded a little suspicious. "Oh, I see. Well, Tina is standing in front of me. Why don't you call me about eight-thirty on Monday? I have to go. Goodbye, Stan." She hung up quickly before her voice cracked.

After disconnecting, she stared at the receiver. It was going to be a very long weekend.

Chapter 11

*A*fter Geeter's comment, everyone fell silent. He cleared his throat. "My favorite memory of Dad was when I's gettin' better from my bullet wounds. Had feelin' in my legs but couldn't move 'em. I was so in love with Kelly and wanted her as my wife, but if I couldn't walk, it weren't gonna happen. I'd be less than a man. Kelly was at a doctor's appointment and I was sittin' alone watchin' TV."

He walked toward the window, and stared outside. "Dad came in, carryin' cheesesteak subs he made for us. We had a long talk. Asked me if'n I had somethin' to ask him. I said no and he laughed, right in my face sayin' I was a liar. I asked what he meant and he said he knew I wanted to marry Kelly."

Geeter turned to face the family. " 'Just ask me,' he said. I replied, 'I cain't, not if I can't move my legs. I'm not a real man.' He grabbed my arms and shook me. 'Quit feeling sorry for yourself, son. A man is more than what he can do physically. It's what he does emotionally. Kelly's happier than ever, only because of you and the love you share. Her children love you. Mom and I love you.' Then he said something that rocked my world. 'Even if you never take another step, you're more of a man than anyone else I've ever met. You saved the lives of two of my daughters and three of my grandchildren through your selfless act of showing up when Ballister had a gun pointed at them'."

Geeter stopped to paw at his eyes again. "Told me even if'n I didn't marry Kelly, he'd still think of me as his son. Then he asked if I was really sure there wasn't anything I wanted to ask him. Right there and then, I asked for Kelly's hand in marriage." Geeter let out a belly laugh. "Know what Dad said? 'I'll think about it. Get back to you soon.' He walked out of the room! I sat there thinkin' 'What the...'. Then he came back thirty seconds later with two beers. 'Geeter, I'll gladly give my blessin' for you to marry Kelly.' "

Geeter's jaw started quivering. He turned to the window so the others couldn't see his face.

***

It was also a very long and lonely weekend for Stan. Los Angeles was no longer his home. Further complicating matters was whatever had happened between him and Nora. As he took a walk, his mind replayed the conversation over and over. There was something she wasn't saying. He wasn't sure what it was, but he could have sworn she was about to cry when she'd suddenly hung up. He began to wonder if Martina was really calling her or if she just used that as an excuse to get off the line.

Stan stopped to cross the intersection, deep in thought about their relationship. Despite the comfort he had given Nora about finding a way for their friendship to continue, he knew it would come to a screeching halt. But it would be her marriage to what's his name, not his relocation that would end it. When Nora got married, Stan wouldn't be able to see her, to call her, to do nice things for her. He wandered aimlessly on the way back to the hotel.

Stan studied his face in the motel room mirror, searching for a solution. He knew he should just bow out now and prevent the major heartbreak that would come when she said her vows. But as much as his mind told him to walk away, his heart wouldn't permit it. He tried to understand. What the hell was wrong with him?

It suddenly occurred to Stan. The problem was that he was in love with Nora. *This can't be.* How could he love someone so much when he knew that a love between them would never work out? It made him so sad that he couldn't sleep either Saturday or Sunday nights. He couldn't fathom why he was drawn to Nora. His need for her was on a scale of needing to breathe. He couldn't help it, no matter how much he tried. He knew he should leave her alone, but he couldn't. This wouldn't end well for him, but he was powerless to stop it.

The time between their conversation on Thursday night and his call on Monday seemed to drag on for weeks. He counted the minutes until eight-thirty. Finally it was time to call Nora. But it rang and rang. There was no answer. Stan grew concerned. He kept trying, calling every few minutes for almost two hours before he gave up. He was panicked something bad had happened. Anxiety filled his soul as his mind tried to come up with a reason she wasn't answering.

Despite his concern, he waited until the next morning before calling again. He considered the possibility that she just didn't want to talk to him, but that wasn't like her. Again, he wondered if it had something to do with the way she'd acted the last time they spoke.

He knew he should just forget about her, but he also had to know she was all right. Logically, he decided to call before Nora took the girls to school. His reasoning was even if she didn't want to talk to him, it would be hard not to answer the phone with her daughters there.

Cassandra answered on the second ring, "Hello? Crittendale residence."

With relief in his heart and his voice, he said, "Cassie, is that you? This is Stan. How are you doing? Is everything all right?"

There was genuine happiness in her voice, "Stan, hi! Are you coming over today?"

"No, honey. I'm in California. May I please speak to your mommy?"

Cassandra didn't bother to cover the receiver. When she screamed for her mom, Stan thought he might lose his hearing permanently.

Nora came on shortly. "Hello?"

"Nora, it's Stan. Is everything okay?"

There was annoyance in her voice. "Yes, why wouldn't it be?"

"I tried to call you last night, but you didn't answer. I was worried sick that something happened to you or one of the girls."

"No, nothing happened. I just didn't feel like talking. That *was* all right, wasn't it?" She said it with an air of superiority, like she was either better than he was or else she was very, very upset. It was a tone he hadn't heard from her since that day on the porch on Elm Street. That confirmed it. He must've done something to offend her, but didn't have a clue what it was.

"Did I do something wrong, Nora?"

She sighed. "No, not at all. Why do you ask?"

"No reason, I guess. You just seem different, that's all. May I call you tonight?"

"Stan, you must be spending a fortune on these calls. Let's not do this for a while."

He was crushed. Something was going on! "Please talk to me, Nora. Let me in, please?"

"I don't have time to talk. I'm just about to head out the door to take the girls to school. We can talk on Friday when you come over for supper."

He didn't like her attitude. "I'm not sure you want me to come over."

There was definite anger in her voice. "Of course I do. Now, may I ask you a favor?"

Maybe this would reveal what was wrong, "Sure. Anything."

"Would you mind babysitting the girls on Saturday and Sunday night? I need to get some evening hours in if I'm going to keep my finances afloat."

Well, that definitely wasn't what he had hoped for. But he liked the girls and wanted to help Nora out. "Of course. I'd be glad to watch them."

"Good. I'll schedule my shifts. On Friday, we'll go over what you need to do. I appreciate it. Goodbye, Stan." She hung up.

He stood there lost in thought. What had he done?

Stan moped for the rest of the week. He played and replayed their conversations over and over in his mind, but didn't see any reason for her to be angry with him. What had he done? *What does it really matter?* In a few short months, she would be Tim's wife.

***

Back in the apartment, Nora turned to her girls. "Okay ladies, get your things together. Don't forget to grab your lunches."

Cassandra whined, "Did you make tuna fish sandwiches again, Mommy?"

Nora answered sharper than she really meant. "It's all we have! At least be thankful you have something to eat."

Cassandra turned away, obviously hurt.

Little Martina looked at her mother's face. "Mommy, why are you crying?"

Nora wiped her eyes. "Never you mind, little miss. Get your coats on! We don't want to be late. It's rude to be late."

***

Stan's flight got in just after noon on Friday. Detroit had their first real snowfall of the season. He had a hard time keeping the Corvette on the road. When he slid through an intersection and almost collided with another vehicle, he knew he couldn't drive the sports car in this type of weather anymore. He needed something else for safety. *That's why I purchased the Tahoe.*

He shook his head. A small part of him felt that if Nora wanted to act like this, he should just take his Chevy back. But the rest of him said that wouldn't be fair to her. He stopped at a dealership on the way from the airport and traded in his Vette for an S-10 Blazer. He no longer needed the speedster anyway. He'd only purchased the hot rod because Linda loved them so much. Well, she was no longer in his life, so what did the kind of car he drove really matter anymore? The dealership told him they'd prepare the Blazer and paperwork so he could pick up his new car the next day.

He arrived at Nora's apartment Friday evening. While the reception the girls gave him was wonderful, Nora's response was icy cold. She barely spoke to him during the meal. Before clearing the dishes, she went over the directions about what she wanted him to do when babysitting the girls.

He shook his head. "Giving them a bath? That's out of the question."

Her lips set in a white line. "Fine."

After their discussion was over, she stood up. "Stan, I need to get the girls ready for bed now, so why don't you plan on being here about one-thirty? I need to be at work by two and will be there until eleven. Fine with you?"

He remained silent for a second. "Yes. That'll be great. But before I leave, would you please tell me what I did to offend or upset you?"

"You didn't do anything, Stanley. Why do you keep saying that?"

He answered warily, "I don't know. Something changed. The last time you called me Stanley was when I came to see you when you were sick back in high school. Then you didn't want to talk this past week, and now tonight you barely said two words to me during dinner. Was your week bad? Is that it?"

"Other than barely making enough to make it worth my while to go in, it was fine. Look, I really have to get moving. I also need to tidy the apartment and do the dishes."

"Would you like some help?"

"No. You've done more than enough. I appreciate your generosity and willingness to watch the girls this weekend. This is only temporary until I find a permanent sitter."

He reached for her hand, taking it softly. "You know I don't mind helping you out with anything, don't you?"

She looked down at where he held her hand for a long moment. Softly, she pulled her hand away. "I know, Stan, but there is a lot more to your life than helping us. You had better go. Goodnight."

He didn't want the evening to end with the distance between them. "Nora, please talk to me, I feel like..."

She quickly opened the door and motioned for him to leave. "I need you to leave. Goodnight!" He stood there looking at her eyes, which appeared to be about to tear. "Stan, please? Just leave."

He nodded and left.

As instructed, Stan arrived precisely at one-thirty. Nora's demeanor was even cooler than the previous night. The girls, however, were so happy to see him. They had a whole evening of activities planned. Before they got too involved, Stan looked at Nora's directions for supper. It called for one box of macaroni and cheese with a can of tuna folded in. That was what she had made the previous evening for dinner.

A thought entered his mind. "Cassie, do you like tuna fish?"

Both girls came running over to him. Cassandra answered, "No. I hate it. Mommy packs tuna fish sandwiches every day for lunch. I'm sick of it. We have macaroni and cheese with tuna fish almost every night. I hate that, too."

Little Martina chimed in, "I hates spoona-fish!"

Stan laughed. These girls were so adorable. "Ladies, get your coats. We're going shopping!" Nora was already pissed at him and this was going to make it worse. Oh well, may as well make sure the girls had a nutritious meal in their bellies. It'd be worth it.

The girls liked the new mini-Blazer a lot. This one had power windows that Cassandra couldn't quit playing with. Martina whined, as only a pretty little five year old can do.

"S'not fair. Cassie's playing with my window. My turn."

Stan took it all in and his heart filled with happiness. He realized he loved the girls, too. Both Chevy's had cassette players. He'd bought a couple of tapes in California. One of them was *The Muppet Show Cast Album*. His two young charges were big Muppet fans and before long, they were all singing along. "Grandma's Feather Bed" was their favorite song.

The grocery store was glad to see Stan and the girls come... well, at least the manager was. The cashier and baggers were glad to see them leave. Two heaping carts of groceries were the result of the trip. Nora's cupboards and fridge were jam packed with food. Where Nora's freezer had only contained a couple of old ice trays, it was now completely stocked with meats, veggies, a few quick-cook meals and even ice cream.

"So what do you want for supper?"

"Fried chicken," Martina answered.

Stan made Shake 'n Bake, homemade mashed potatoes with mushroom gravy, carrots with brown sugar and crescent rolls. Then he fed the girls chocolate cake and ice cream for dessert.

Before bedtime, Stan and the girls went on a safari to the laundry room. It took several trips to get the five loads of laundry finished. Stan had purchased the classic Doctor Seuss book, *Green Eggs and Ham,* and read to them before bedtime. His heart was touched when Cassandra told him she wouldn't be able to sleep unless he gave her a goodnight kiss. Stan softly kissed both girls' heads before he turned off the lights. He was glad when he closed the door because he didn't have to explain the tears in his eyes.

Stan had two hours before Nora got back home. He put it to good use. By the time he heard Nora's key in the lock, all the dishes were washed, the apartment was straightened up and all the laundry was folded, with the exception of undergarments. Her dinner was warming in the oven. He didn't want a conflict, so he quickly donned his coat.

The door swung open and there stood Nora. She looked so tired. Her uniform was stained. The mascara around her eyes was streaked, as if she had been crying. His heart went out to her. "Welcome home. How was your day?"

She closed the door and kicked off her shoes. "Very long. Had a few extremely rude customers. But I did make a couple of good tips." She pulled a small handful of bills from her pocket. "How much do I owe you for watching the girls?"

He frowned. "Absolutely nothing. Don't talk so funny!"

Her face turned red. "I am not going to accept charity from you. If you don't let me pay, I will be pissed!"

Stan smiled. *Wait until you open your cabinets.*

She held out a twenty. "How much?"

"Nothing. I don't want your money."

She became very upset. "If you can't accept my money, you can't watch the girls anymore! Don't believe me? Try me, just go ahead."

Stan didn't want that, but she was beginning to offend him. "Okay. How about ten dollars?" He would use that money to put gas in the Tahoe or buy the girls something.

She coolly handed him two fives. "By the way, I didn't see your Corvette outside. Everything okay?"

He had to be careful here. "It was time to get rid of it. I traded it in on something more practical."

The anger changed to concern in her face. "But I thought you loved that car? What did you exchange it for?"

"I now own an S-10 Blazer. The weather up here is a lot worse than Southern California. This will go much better in the snow."

Her face paled. "That was why you bought the Tahoe, wasn't it? My neediness forced you to get rid of the car you loved. I'm sorry. It seems..." She got quiet as she brushed her arm across her eyes.

"It's no big deal, really it isn't. It was only a car and the reason I had to hold onto the Vette doesn't exist anymore."

Her ears perked up as she stared at his face. "What does that mean?"

Crap! He had to extricate himself out of the conversation before he said something stupid. "Oh, I'm just getting older, you know—more mature. It's time for me to grow up. Look, I'm tired and I need to leave. Goodnight, Nora. See you tomorrow."

***

Nora quickly turned out the lights and watched him climb into the red and black mini-Blazer. After he left, she turned on the lights. Something about what he said, specifically about the reason about not holding onto the Vette anymore, bothered her. She wondered if he and Linda were having problems. Could it be she was the reason?

Her mind was focused on her thoughts until she opened the refrigerator door to look for something to eat. For the first time since she'd moved to this apartment, it was totally stocked! She opened the kitchen cupboards and they were filled to overflowing as well. Then she noticed it—the luscious scent of food cooking in her oven. There in aluminum foil were two fried chicken legs, potatoes and gravy, crescent rolls and vegetables.

After Nora placed the food on the table, her head was spinning. How could it be that Stan could do all these nice things for her when he was married to someone else? Why couldn't this be real for her? As she looked around, she noticed all the dishes had been washed, dried and put away. A laundry basket sat on the floor, containing only underclothes for her and the girls. She walked into her bedroom to find everything else already folded. All of her waitress uniforms were neatly hung on hangers.

She stumbled back to the kitchen. *Why would he do this?* As she devoured the food, she pondered that question. Two distinct possibilities floated to the top.

Nora tried to call Stan at his apartment that night and several times during the day, with no luck. She didn't know whether to be cross at him or thankful. She hoped he would come early on Sunday so they could talk, but he arrived just in time for her to leave. When she got home that evening, Stan was already packed, waiting to go.

"I didn't get a chance to thank you for the groceries and having my dinner prepared last night. That was very nice."

"Just trying to be kind to an old friend."

"Why don't we sit and talk for a while?"

His eyes didn't meet hers. "Can't. I have to get some shut eye. Full slate of meetings tomorrow. Phase one of planning for next year's budget."

She tried not to let her disappointment show. "I see."

His coat was on. When he reached the door, he turned. "Need me to babysit this week? Your girls are so nice. Be glad to do it."

"You wouldn't mind?"

"No, not at all."

"Would Friday, Saturday and Sunday evenings be okay?"

"Yep. See you then. 'Night."

Something about his hasty departure wasn't right. Maybe he was trying to play head games with her.

After he left, she found dinner was again waiting in the oven. This time it was some tasty type of fish with a cheesy breaded topping. A twice-baked potato along with little peas and onions in a cream sauce filled out the meal. As she opened the fridge to place her leftovers in it, her mouth dropped open.

Stan had meals pre-prepared for the entire week. There were directions on how long to bake everything. Also, she saw he had packed lunches for the girls—even cutting the crust off the bread.

She stood staring at the fridge in disbelief. Never had anyone, not even Bob, treated her like this. She said a prayer to God thanking Him for sending Stan, then said a prayer she was not proud of afterwards. She asked God to *somehow* bring Stan into her life as more than a friend.

***

Nora tried to call Stan dozens of time during the week, but he didn't answer. She thought he was angry with her for not telling him why she'd been cross. She wished he'd just forget it. Nora missed the way things used to be between them. They had to get past this or she would go insane.

Nora pondered what to do. She decided that if he wouldn't answer her calls at home, she'd call him at work. On Thursday afternoon, the restaurant was slow. Nora looked up the number for Stan's office, dialing him on the pay phone behind the corner booth.

"Stanley Jenkins' office," the receptionist answered. "May I help you?"

"Uh, yes. May I speak to Stan, I mean Mr. Jenkins?"

"Let me see if he's available. May I ask who's calling?"

"Yes," she hesitated just a little. "It's Nora, Nora Crittendale."

"Just a moment, ma'am. Let me see if he'll take your call."

Nora only had to wait a few seconds before Stan's voice came on the line. She could hear the anxiety and worry. "Nora, everything okay? Something wrong with you or the girls?"

"Oh no, Stan! I've just tried to call you a couple of times this week and you didn't answer." She cleared her throat. "So, I, uh, wanted to find out what time you would be available on Friday evening."

Stan sighed. "So glad everything's okay. Be there at one-thirty, just like on the weekend."

That was surprising. "Won't you get in trouble, I mean, leaving early?"

His laugh reminded her of summer sunshine. She realized how much she missed the sound of it. For whatever reason, butterflies tickled her belly.

"Nora, maybe I wasn't clear about this, but you should know, I am *the* boss here."

It was her turn to laugh. "Well, if you're really sure about that..."

"Wait, let me see. I am looking at the sign above my door. Yep, it says Stanley Jenkins, top dog and main boss."

"If you say so," she snickered. "Sounds like you're in a good mood. Any particular reason?"

He hesitated before answering. "Yes, there is. This is the longest and most pleasant conversation we've had in a long time."

"Is that a fact? Well, why don't you plan on coming over early on Saturday and we can talk more."

"That's a possibility, but first, you have to do something for me."

Great. What would he ask her to do? Part of her fear was that there were strings attached. With Tim, there were always strings attached. She regretted most of the things Tim attached strings to.

"Still there?"

"Yes, sorry. What do I have to do, Stan?"

He drew a loud and deep breath. "It's quite simple. Tell me what I did to upset you."

She certainly didn't want to talk about it. "What do you mean?"

The frivolity had left his voice. "You know exactly what I mean. Something happened between us. I need to know what it was so I can understand it."

Now she regretted calling him. "Stan..."

"Look, I don't expect much from our friendship, but honesty is one of the things I want and need. How can you be my best friend when you can't even be honest with me?"

The entire conversation was now annoying her. In anger, she blurted, "You're the one who called us best friends."

Stan was silent. His silence concerned her. As soon as the words left her lips, she regretted saying them. It was a while before she added, "I didn't mean that the way it came out, Stan. Of course you're my best friend. You do know that, don't you?"

Stan's voice was now tinged with ice. "Nora, I have a budget meeting in ten minutes and I need to review the ledgers so I'm prepared. I'll be at your place at one-thirty tomorrow afternoon."

"Stan, don't go, not like this. I didn't mean to say what I did. I didn't mean to hurt you. Please forgive me."

"I have to go, Nora. Goodbye."

He hung up, but Nora didn't want their conversation to end, not like this. She pulled another dime from her apron and inserted it into the coin slot. She asked to speak with Stan but was forwarded to his secretary, whose name was Gwen. Gwen told Nora to hold on while she checked if he was available. Nora knew she'd hurt him, but so many things were running through her mind she'd been confused.

Gwen's voice caught her attention. "Mrs. Crittendale?"

"Yes?"

"Mr. Jenkins isn't available right now. He asked me to tell you he will be tied up for the rest of the day."

"Thank you."

The secretary's voice was chipper, as if she were smiling. "Mr. Jenkins really does have a busy schedule today. Frankly, I was surprised he took your call earlier. Why don't you try him some other time?"

"Yes, yes, of course you're right. I'm sorry. Thanks for your help. Goodbye."

"Have a pleasant day, Mrs. Crittendale."

After hanging up the phone, Nora intentionally banged her head against the side of the phone booth so hard that she immediately developed a headache. She hadn't intended to hurt him, but she knew she had. She cursed at herself.

A customer walked past her, heading to the restroom. Stan had been right. He was her best friend, back then, now, and probably the best friend she'd ever have in her entire life. No one had ever cared or done as much for her as Stan. He talked to her, listened to her, bent over backwards to help her. Made her feel good about herself. It was so obvious that he cared, not by his words but by his actions.

She entered the restroom, blew her nose and washed her hands. He did a hell of a lot more than Tim—and she was *engaged* to Tim. There was always a cost with her fiancé. Was there one with Stan? There had to be, what with all he was doing for her. Nothing in life was free. But what was Stan's angle? What did he want from her? And would she be willing to pay it?

***

As promised, Stan arrived promptly at one-thirty. The girls had gotten out of school early and were in the apartment when he arrived. Martina seemed so endeared with him, staring up with those big brown eyes that melted his heart. She'd been watching for him at the window.

Stan waved when he heard her rapping against the glass, happily yelling to him. Before Stan could open the exterior door, Cassandra had the apartment door open. The girls ran down the hallway, clinging to him as soon as he reached the top of the stairs. He entered her apartment with Nora's daughters being held tightly, one in each arm.

Stan nodded at Nora before asking if there were any special instructions for the evening. Nora shook her head and gave each daughter a kiss. She met Stan's gaze for a moment, but left without saying a word. He couldn't read her expression, but it didn't look good.

That afternoon, Stan took the girls to the library. One of the librarians led story time, reading a few children's books Stan hadn't heard of before. When they left, both little ladies had library cards and a stack of books. After getting the girls to promise not to tell, he took them to a Dairy Queen for a fudge sundae.

Nora returned home a few minutes later than normal. Stan had started to worry, but his fears left when he heard her key in the lock. Just like the previous weekend, she looked absolutely exhausted. Her hair was askew, makeup smeared and eyes heavy with exhaustion. Stan had planned on leaving immediately, but decided to stay for a few moments. He helped her to the sofa and massaged her feet after slipping off her waitress shoes.

"We had tacos for dinner. Fix you a plate?"

Her eyes studied his. "That'd be sweet."

He returned shortly with the meal and a glass of sweet tea.

She continued to study him while she ate.

Life is so rough on her. I wish...

Her face was expressionless as she said, "Thanks for everything today. The girls love it when you watch them. What did you do?"

"We went to the library, then played games—Chutes and Ladders, Old Maid and Go Fish to be exact. Then they helped me make dinner. Your girls are so sweet and so much fun. Cassie told me her class has been studying Eskimos in school. She and Tina were practicing rubbing noses. In fact, we rubbed noses to say goodnight."

Nora's face was filled with sadness as she nodded. Probably wasn't overly happy about the way Stan and the girls bonded. Stan picked up on the sadness. "Nora, sorry I couldn't take your second call yesterday. I feel like there is an obstacle between us. Please, let's get it out into the open and get past it. Our time together is so limited. I don't want to squander it with some petty issue."

Nora bristled. "So now my feelings are petty?"

"I didn't say that. But whether it's petty or major, I'm afraid we won't be able to get past whatever is wrong unless we talk about it."

"And if I don't want to talk about it?"

Stan sighed, shaking his head. "I think it's time for me to go."

"So, is this how it's going to be? As soon as I don't want to talk about what you want to talk about, you leave?"

He stared at her. When had their friendship turned into this mire of, of whatever it was? "Okay, I'll bite. What would you like to talk about?"

She fumbled over the words. "I don't know, anything!"

"Like what?"

"I don't care. You pick a subject."

It was time to address the elephant in the room. "Nora, let me be perfectly frank with you. You are the closest friend I've ever had. Not knowing what's wrong... what *I* did wrong... this is killing me! Please, I'm begging you. Tell me what's going on inside that pretty little head of yours."

She stared at him, just shaking her head. He knew something was happening in her mind. Something monumental. Perhaps it was time for him to just leave and never come back. He waited almost five minutes for her to say something, anything. Stan read the hesitation in her eyes as not wanting to speak with him. He simply nodded, stood up and retrieved his coat. He had nothing else to say to her except, "I'll see you at one-thirty tomorrow. Goodnight."

He was almost at the door when the softness of her voice surprised him. "Are you and Linda having problems?"

He quickly whipped around to stare at her. He couldn't believe what he saw. Tears were slowly staining her cheeks. He fought the urge to wipe them away. "No, why would you ask?"

"Our relationship is causing the problem, isn't it?" Before he could answer, she added, "And don't lie to me, Stan. I also need your honesty. What's wrong is I'm scared of many things. The first is that I'm causing problems in your married life."

He threw his coat against the wall. "I can honestly say that you, the girls and our friendship are not causing any problems whatsoever in my life with Linda."

She gave him a questioning look. "I don't understand. You're married, but you spend more time with me than you do with her. How can that not be a problem?"

His mind was running in circles. Should he tell her his marriage was over? Should he tell her how he really felt? He wanted to tell her the truth, but if he did, what would happen? Maybe she'd tell him to get lost. Maybe she'd limit their friendship. Or maybe, just maybe, above all hopes, she'd confess she felt the same and they would live happily ever after. Maybe she'd dump Tim and spend every second of her life with him. But what if...

"Before I answer that question, let me ask one in reverse. You spend more time with me than you do with Tom..."

He had known her fiancé's name, but he got it wrong intentionally as an insult, not to Nora, but to Tim. She saw right through it. "His name is Tim, not Tom, but you knew that, didn't you?"

"Yeah, guess I did. Tim, Tom, Bill, I don't care what his name is, all I know is that he'll be the one sitting next to you in a rocking chair at the end of your life. I need to know if he'll make you happy, that's all."

***

Nora stared into his eyes, contemplating how to respond. Would she ever be happy with Tim? Maybe, but that was doubtful. Tim had his flaws, and while she hoped he'd overcome them, she had her doubts. Her mind knew what she really wanted. Her hope for happiness was the pipe dream of a love with Stan.

Suppose she expressed it out loud? Three things could happen: A, the situation between them might not change; B, he could be offended and end their relationship immediately; or C, he might leave Linda for her and they'd live out a fairy tale. *C! C! Please be C!* Her heart begged her to go for C. But even if it was true, someone would lose out. Her happiness would come at someone else's expense. Could she live with that? All of her, including her heart, screamed no.

What she was about to say was a lie. "Tim makes me very, very happy. Look, I don't feel comfortable talking about him with you. I also get the distinct feeling you aren't comfortable talking about Linda with me. So let's agree that those subjects are just taboo. Let's not talk about them, okay?"

***

Stan felt a chill slowly creep down his body. *She is in love with him.* He had hoped she would tell him she wasn't happy. If she gave him an indication, any indication at all, he would pour out every feeling he'd been holding back. His gut told him she wasn't happy, but who was he to know, really know what Nora felt in her heart?

She smiled when he nodded his head, but her expression changed. "Since we're being honest, I need to ask one more thing. This is going to be difficult, but I want honesty. Before I ask it, will you promise to tell me the truth?"

"Of course I will."

"Promise?"

"Yes, I promise."

"Will you promise on our friendship?"

His heart had already been torn apart by her telling him Tim made her very, very happy. What else could there be? The hurt was so bad he was becoming physically ill. He answered, "Yes. I promise on our friendship."

"Okay," she took a deep breath, as she studied his face intensely. "Stan, you treat me so nice. And not just me, but the girls, too. You gave me your new car to use. You stocked my apartment with food. You cook, clean, shop, tidy up and generally make my life easier. But above all else, you give me something I've needed and wanted. You gave me your unconditional friendship."

She stood, walking to face him. "Since Bob died, I've come to realize people don't just do nice things for no reason at all. Everyone has an angle. Not a damn thing in life is free."

The way she said that made him feel so sorry for her. There was something she had been through she wasn't telling him and he could see in her eyes it had been horrible.

"So, I need to know. What's the price of your friendship? Are you doing this out of hope I'll give you something in return? If that's the case, you certainly deserve anything you want. If that's your game and you did it to get me into bed, you earned it. I'll repay my debt. Let's get it over."

His mouth dropped open. Stan was so mad he was seeing red. With anger, he replied, "Dammit! If that's the type of person you think I am, you don't know me at all! How could you... Do you really think the only reason I helped you was to get you into bed? Never knew you thought so little of me. This is unbelievable!" His hands trembled as he turned toward the door.

She grabbed his arm. "Then what's the price? Nothing is free, so tell me. What do I owe you in return?"

He was still angered, but the feel of her hand on his arm kept him from making a nasty response. "I don't know what you have been through, Nora, but let me tell you this. Everything I did, I did for you. I only did it because I wanted to. I never once expected a single damn thing in return and even if you'd offer, I'd never take anything from you. I only wanted your friendship."

Her eyes searched his, as if she were boring into his mind. His anger was turning to disappointment. His actions had been misinterpreted.

"Everything I did was out of friendship. You have two choices. Think of me like everyone else or just accept the fact that maybe someone does something nice for you, without having a price tag attached simply because you're you." He turned and picked up his coat.

Before he could turn back toward her, she wrapped him in her arms. "I didn't think you were like that, but I had to know. I had to ask and offer, had to find out if you really were like other men. But you aren't!"

This was too much for Stan. On his lips, his confession of love for her was about to spill out. He needed to leave. He wriggled from her embrace, said goodnight and left.

***

Nora turned out the lights and ran to the window. She watched him climb into his car and leave. There was something in his eyes, something he was holding back. Tonight had been a gamble, a gamble to see how much he really cared. Now she knew. Their friendship was built on trust. Trust and... what?

She turned the lights back on and ate her tacos. Why did he go to all the trouble to do these things for her? The answer filled her mind. Despite being married to Linda, Stan loved her.

They settled into a somewhat comfortable pattern over the last weeks of November. Stan watched her two little girls. She knew he spoiled them as often as he could. He'd become their father figure. Cassandra and Martina loved and adored him. He was all either one of them spoke about. And he was all she could think about. She cried herself to sleep every night wishing they could be together. But when she was with him, she acted like nothing was wrong.

***

It was getting harder and harder to do this and not tell her. Not tell her she was making a mistake. He cursed Tim. Yes, it was wrong, but why couldn't Tim seriously screw up or just die? But Stan refused to tell her. Instead, he lied to her, acting like nothing was wrong out of fear of hurting Nora.

On Thanksgiving morning, Nora had to work, so Stan watched the girls. Nora asked him not to do anything special that day. She wanted to take them all out to dinner. Of course, Stan planned to ignore her request.

He walked her out to the Tahoe, wishing her a good day when she left for work at five-thirty. As soon as she was out of sight, he retrieved the groceries he'd brought along. He allowed the girls to sleep in until the luscious scent of honey baked ham brought them into the kitchen. While he worked on the filling and mashed potatoes, he watched them eat the chocolate chip pancakes he made just for them.

Nora walked in the door at two. She stared at the wonderfully prepared meal waiting on the table.

"What's this?"

"Surprise. We made a feast for you. Doesn't it smell good?"

He could sense her anger, saw her eyes smolder. "You know I wanted to take us out to dinner."

"But your girls and I..."

"No. This is you. This is about control."

All the happiness at seeing her walk in the door left. She was angry because of her pride. She'd saved enough to treat them all to supper and he'd ruined it. He sensed the girls watching. Couldn't risk a fight in front of them.

"I just wanted to do something nice for you. But I know you planned to take us out. Sorry I ruined that." Her jaw was set. She was pissed. Inside he chuckled. No matter what she did, she couldn't help it. She was drop dead gorgeous. But now wasn't the time to think about that. *Screwed this up.*

Stan grabbed his coat from the back of the couch. He lied, "Got some work I brought home I need to do. I'll head out now. See you tomorrow morning."

Cassandra and Martina grabbed his hands. Martina looked at him with those big brown eyes. "Don't go, Stan. You promised to wishbone with me."

Nora's voice commanded his attention. "Wishbone with you?"

"You know. Promised Tina she and I would see who got their wish." *Know what my wish would be.*

He stooped to hug the girls. "Happy Thanksgiving. Remember to listen to your mommy."

Stan stood and turned to her. Her expression wasn't as severe as before, but... "Happy Thanksgiving, Nora."

Nora shook her head. "I want you to know I'm disappointed in you."

Stan hung his head. "I'm sorry. I screwed up."

"That's not why I'm disappointed."

"No?"

"No. I thought you were a man of your word."

"I am."

"Then you better stay. A certain someone is waiting to see who gets their wish." A smile wiped across her face, like sunshine after a thunderstorm.

"I'd like that."

She nodded her head quickly. "Me too."

It turned out to be the best Thanksgiving he'd ever had.

Nora was scheduled for the early shift the next morning on Black Friday. Stan and the girls drove her to work. They were waiting for her when she got off. Stan drove them to a tree farm where they picked out a beautiful Blue Spruce. While the girls clapped and danced, Stan chopped it down. The four of them sang Christmas songs as they dragged the tree back to the cashier's station.

While the tree farm workers tied their selection to the top of the Tahoe, Stan had to excuse himself. He was suddenly overcome with emotion. He felt it coming on and didn't want the girls to see his tears. This was love. The love of a family, his dream. This was everything he'd ever wanted and needed in life. These girls were the ones he wanted as his own, the girls he loved. Being with them made him so happy, but life was cruel. This wouldn't be his happiness. Next year, it would be Tim and Nora, not Stan and Nora, picking out a tree together. He looked to heaven. *Why? Why are You doing this to me?* This was absolute torture! A small voice within him softly whispered, *"You have the choice to walk away."* He bitterly answered back, *"No, I don't. My girls need me."*

He was wiping his cheeks when Nora came looking for him. He could see the concern in her eyes. "Tell me what's wrong," she said.

I can't. Not the truth. He quickly brushed his tears away as he lied, "Just thinking how it will be when I have a family someday. Being with the three of you makes me wish it was today."

Nora turned away, but not before he had seen her tears. Apparently she felt it, too. They stood in silence. It took every bit of his resolve not to hold her in his arms and tell her how he really felt. Stan wished and prayed the situation was different, but it wasn't. Nora belonged to Tim.

On the drive back to Nora's apartment, they stopped at a mall to let the girls visit with Santa. They hadn't spoken since she found him at the tree farm. When the girls were in line, Nora suddenly turned toward him. She took Stan's hand, squeezing it very tightly.

Nora's voice quivered. "I have two things I need to say. First, I wanted to tell you I'm sorry for testing you a couple of weeks ago. That was so wrong of me. I apologize. Can you forgive me?"

The warmth of her hand in his was intense. She could have brought him up on a charge of treason and he wouldn't have cared. "Of course I forgive you. What's the second thing?"

Stan noticed she was blushing.

"I wanted to thank you. For everything. For how you've showered the girls and me with your kindness. You're a godsend. I'm so thankful you came back into my life."

Nora turned toward him, her lips so inviting. He couldn't fight it anymore, the urge to hold her. He held his arms open. She stepped forward, wrapping her own around his waist. Her touch was light, making his skin tingle. He was beginning to lose restraint.

The look in her eyes was one he had never seen before. Was that the look of love? He wanted to kiss those lips, taste her and hold her until eternity passed away. She touched the back of his neck, softly pulling his lips toward hers. Stan's heart was going to burst. He lowered his mouth to hers. Nora's breath was warm, the essence of tangerines and cinnamon. But as their lips were just about to touch, Martina grabbed Nora's arm.

"Mommy! Mommy! Santa gave me an orange and a candy cane! See?"

Nora pulled away from Stan to pick up her daughter. Stan turned and walked away. *What the hell am I doing? I almost gave in to lust.* He glanced at Nora. She was staring at him intensely with concern in her eyes. The pain in his heart was killing him. Stan felt that maybe he should just walk outside and jump in front of a bus. Nora was getting married soon and here he had almost given in to his desires. No matter how much he wanted her, he couldn't do this. This wasn't fair to her! He had almost taken advantage of Nora in the name of their friendship.

***

The distance following their near kiss confirmed it. She'd pushed the envelope. Gone over the line. She'd tempted a married man. This couldn't happen again. Stan had made it clear there were no strings attached in their relationship. He said he didn't want anything, nor should she.

They ignored each other for the rest of the time at the mall. Arriving back at the apartment, Stan mounted the tree in the holder.

"I'm tired. Think I'll head out."

The girls were busy watching an animated show on TV. Nora turned to him. "Before you leave, sit with me a moment."

"Okay." They walked to the table and sat across from each other.

"I think we need to talk about what happened at the mall, Stan."

He dropped his gaze to avoid eye contact. "I'm sorry, I was totally out of line. Shouldn't have tried to kiss you. I promise it won't ever, ever happen again."

She studied his eyes, though they were looking at the table, not her. "I was going to apologize to you, Stan. I shouldn't have wanted you to kiss me, you know..." Her voice trailed off. Nora was glad he wasn't making eye contact because she was sure he'd notice she was upset.

He frowned, but still didn't look in her direction. "Glad we came to our senses, huh?"

No, she wasn't glad at all, but she forced a smile. "Yeah, me too. Almost made the mistake of our lives, didn't we?"

Stan looked so uncomfortable, like he'd start crying. He sniffed hard, dug at his eyes with the heel of his hand. He looked away. "I agree. We dodged a bullet tonight. Hey, I'm heading out now." He quickly stood and walked to where the girls were watching TV. He grabbed both of them in a gigantic hug.

Now Nora was confused! What was going on? Stan did think the kiss was a mistake, didn't he? Or did he wish they would have kissed? Was he leaving because she said it was a mistake? And why had he avoided eye contact with her for this entire conversation?

A lump formed in her throat. She tried to hold back her emotions as she watched him kiss Cassandra and Martina goodbye. Then he turned, simply nodding to her before leaving. Stan almost made it out of the door before she saw... running like a stream down his cheeks. He hurried out without saying another word.

Stan's tears left her more confused than ever.

Chapter 12

They sat together, all lost in their own thoughts until Cassandra broke the silence. "Mom, what's your favorite memory of Daddy?"

Nora smiled as she recollected their life together. "I don't know if can pick out one favorite moment in time. Daddy gave me so many mountaintop experiences. Perhaps my favorite was when he took me to Venice for my fortieth birthday. It was one of the rare vacations we took together, just the two of us."

Nora walked to the window. The beauty of a light snow was blanketing the world outside. So pretty, just like the memories floating in her mind. "We sailed in a gondola. It was so romantic. Daddy gave me roses. He brought a bottle of wine, and fed me cheese and grapes. What I remember most..." she had trouble controlling her voice, "...was that during the entire ride, he only looked into my eyes. He ignored the beauty of where we were, giving me all of his attention. I don't know how many times he told me he loved me, cherished me and thanked me for making his life complete. I shouldn't tell you this, but Dad and I made love all night long."

Nora's cheeks warmed as she studied her daughters.

"There are so many things Daddy did to make me feel loved. He always went to work early, but he'd call and sing me awake, every day, even when he was on the road. Your daddy made us the family we are today. Nurtured and loved each one of you. For Tina and Cassie, he was the one who kept the memory of Bob Crittendale alive and made sure Bob's parents stayed active in all four of your lives."

The heartbreak of losing her first husband at such a young age suddenly flooded Nora's mind. Isn't it funny? Stan was her first soulmate, but she lost him. Bob eventually became her soulmate. But then Bob passed away and Stan became her soulmate again. Despite her sorrow, she smiled.

Nora cleared her throat. "Daddy was always so kind to everyone... and he was *fierce* in his love for each of you, his family. He never did things halfway. When he committed, it was one hundred percent. He not only said he loved us, he proved it every day by his actions."

She looked at each of her daughters in turn. "When Daddy came back into my life, he treated me so kindly. After we married, there was never a day I didn't have fresh flowers. Even in horrendous weather he would go out and buy me flowers. When he traveled, he would have them delivered."

The girls exchanged a strange look. Kaitlin walked over to hold her hand. Her voice was gentle. "Momma, you just said 'came back into your life'. Did something happen you haven't told us about?"

"Yes. We intentionally kept it secret from all of you for years."

***

I've got to quit this. He couldn't hide it anymore. Nora was going to see the love in his eyes or pick it up in his voice. Stan knew it was time to start distancing himself from her, but how? *Please God, take this burden from me.*

God answered quickly and loudly.

The laziness of Saturday morning didn't help his problem. Stan had stayed up until the early hours, but couldn't come up with a resolution. Before he drifted off to an uneasy sleep, his bedside clock read five-thirty in the morning. When the phone rang around ten, he was still sleeping.

A very chipper voice greeted him. "Stanley Jenkins! How the heck are you, my friend?"

Stan's head was foggy and he didn't immediately recognize the voice. "Who is this and why are you calling in the middle of the night?"

Laughter filled the telephone line. "I know there's a two-hour time difference between us, but I thought you were ahead of me, not behind. You been drinking this early in the morning?"

Silence followed as Stan tried to identify the caller. The disembodied voice laughed again. "Come on, Stan! It's Joe Summers! Tell me you're not so drunk that you don't remember me!"

Stan shook his head to clear the cobwebs. "I'm sorry. You know I don't drink. You do realize it's Saturday, don't you? Why are you calling me, especially on a holiday weekend?"

Joe laughed. "Now, that's no way for a future vice-president to talk. Where is your dedication, your spirit, your get up and go?"

Stan looked at the phone for a second before laughing. "I think you have the wrong number. You obviously thought you dialed the number of someone who you think gives a crap."

Joe laughed so hard Stan had to move the phone away from his ear. "How've you been, Stan?"

"Fine, Joe. What's up?"

"Not much. Just sitting here drinking a Mimosa, watching the sprinklers water the lawn. Down to business. I need you to free your schedule for December."

"What part?"

"All of it. This thing is happening. The board gave me instructions to get it moving. And I can guarantee you, they'll vote you in overwhelmingly. We need to start thinking about consolidating the smaller labs into the main one in Chicago. Your lab, Stan. We need to do this sooner rather than later. The board wants you to visit all of the smaller facilities, inventory their equipment and decide what we'll keep at those locations for quality control. The rest you can mark to move to your own lab."

Stan rolled onto his back and looked at the overhead light. He allowed his eyes to go out of focus. As he did, he saw Nora's beautiful face. *God, this is going to be hard on her. Probably much harder on me.*

As they talked, Joe sketched out his plan. The company they were buying had six smaller labs in addition to the flagship location in Chicago. The consolidation of equipment would increase the efficiency of the R&D facility in the new company.

They spoke for nearly an hour. After they hung up, Stan realized he'd have very little time to spend with Nora or the girls before he left. He worried about her finances, since he would no longer be able to babysit in the evenings.

I'll run to the bank and withdraw additional money in case she needs it. Stan had been thrifty since high school and had amassed quite a huge sum in savings. He had more than enough to buy a home flat out without financing. *But the house would just be for me.* Hopefully, someday he'd have a family to share it with. He couldn't help but wish it would be Nora and the girls, but Stan wouldn't stand in the way of her happiness.

When he arrived at the apartment that evening, he asked Nora if they could have a serious talk when she got home later. Nora quickly agreed. Stan wondered at the width of her smile. The whole situation was bittersweet. Stan's work dreams were about to come true, but their time together was quickly drawing to an end. He focused on the mission he had planned for the evening.

Stan had very little time to carry out his plan. As soon as Nora left, he bundled up the girls so they could go Christmas shopping. He'd noted Nora's coat had been old and threadbare. She didn't have winter boots either. With the help of Cassandra and Martina, he picked out a heavy winter coat and good, fur-lined winter boots. He allowed the girls to also pick out presents for Mommy before he asked, "What are you two going to ask Santa to bring Mommy?"

Cassandra looked so grown up when she pointed out what Mommy needed. "Mommy needs a new pocket book. She says hers must have a hole because her money doesn't stay in it."

"When I see him, I'll put in a good word. Well... *if* I see him." In his mind, he'd already picked out a gift he knew she could use and cherish. Stan made a mental note which purse to buy when he finished his shopping the next day.

Their next stop was to a toy store. "Girls, why don't you show me what you'll ask Santa for, then you can pick out any book you want." To his surprise, both girls wanted a Cabbage Patch doll. That went into his mental register, too.

Finally, Stan took them to a very nice restaurant for dinner. This would probably be the last time he'd ever take them out.

"Tonight, you can pick anything you want to eat."

Martina stared at him with those big brown eyes. "I want pie with ice cream."

"That's dessert," Cassandra admonished. "Have to eat dinner first."

Stan shook his head. "Not tonight, you don't. Just don't tell Mommy."

Both girls stared at him. Martina twirled her finger in her hair. "Why are you crying?"

Stan quickly brushed his cheeks. "I'm not crying. I have a cold."

Before they went back to the apartment, they stopped at a grocery store to pick out something very special for Nora's dinner.

When he tucked Cassandra and Martina in for the night, he held each of them for a very long time. This was it, possibly the next to last time he'd ever watch them. After bedtime, he did something very sneaky. He went through Nora's bill folder, specifically marking down details on her husband's medical bills.

Then Stan prepared dinner for Nora.

She walked in, kicked off her shoes and hung up her coat. Her smile was so beautiful. How would he be able to live without seeing it every day?

"What is that luscious aroma?"

"My lady." Stan offered his hand and guided her to the table. "Tonight, I offer the bounty of the seas." He brought out a plate of lobster tail, scallops and shrimp. He followed up with a glass of wine.

Her face was flushed. Her smile was from ear to ear. "Is this a special occasion?"

He had to bite his lips to avoid tears. Nora saw his reaction and reached for his hand. He squeezed it tightly. "I have some important news to share with you, but let's eat first."

They dined as she talked about her evening. He shared details of his time with the girls, of course leaving out some very important parts. After the meal, they did dishes together. Stan knew she wasn't just curious about his news, she was anxious as well. They finally sat down at the table.

He studied her face. "I need to tell you what happened early this morning. I got a call from my boss. Don't know how to tell you this, but I'll be travelling the entire month of December."

Her face blanched and her eyes clouded. Her voice was shaky. "Is this... wh-what you w-want?"

No. I want you. He nodded. "Yep."

Nora released his hand and looked away.

He outlined his travel schedule of where he would be and when. She seemed to take it in stride, until he handed her the envelope.

"I know things will be tough financially for you because I won't be here to watch the girls. But this should get you through and make Christmas merry for the three of you."

She opened the envelope to discover $1500 inside. Nora's eyes filled. "I can't accept this, Stan." She tried to hand the envelope back.

Seeing her pretty face wet with tears made his own feel scratchy. He wiped his cheeks with a sleeve before gently pushing the envelope back to her. "You can and you will. I have more than enough money to give this to you. Life has been too rough on you for too long. You need a break. I want you and the girls to have it."

She shook her head. "I will not take a hand-out!"

He gently patted her hand. "Good, because it isn't a hand-out, but rather a hand up. The only thing I ask is someday when you are able, repay the favor by giving something to someone who really needs it."

This was harder than he expected. What he really wanted to tell her was how much he loved her.

Nora buried her head in her hands. It took several minutes to regain her composure. "I don't know what to say. Thanks, Stan. When do you leave?"

"Monday."

Stan stood and walked toward the door. She didn't look at him. It was time to go.

"Guess I'll say goodnight."

"Still watching the girls tomorrow?"

"Of course. Wouldn't miss it."

"I still owe you a meal at a restaurant. Come over at ten tomorrow and we can have our last..." she sobbed hard, "...last meal together."

He reached for her, but she pulled away. So he left. The soft closing of the door was like a jail cell locking. Life as they'd known it had ended.

***

Nora couldn't sleep. She was losing him, *again*. Their time together was almost over. There was so much she wanted to say to him, share with him, to make him understand, but those words would never leave her lips. *Please give me the strength to get through this.*

She had the girls dressed and ready when he arrived. Even though the talk had died down, Nora was still concerned someone might recognize Stan as the Vigilante. She drove the four of them to a restaurant over an hour away. The meal was nice, but inside, she was dying. *This is how a family should be.* The girls loved Stan. He was their hero, the apple of their eyes.

Despite her protest, Stan picked up the bill. He asked Nora to stop at a mall. Stan tried to explain to the girls he would be going away for a while, but they didn't seem to understand. He bought them nice winter coats as a going away present.

When they returned to the Tahoe, Nora turned to him. "I'm gonna call off."

"Why?"

"You know why. I, uh, we won't see you for a while."

He turned his gaze from her to the girls. "It'll go fast. Wanted to spend the night just hanging around your daughters." His eyes met hers. They were vacant. "It's fine, really."

The night seemed to drag on for months. Finally she was on the stairs, key in the lock. The scent of broiled steaks awaited her. The table was set, food steaming. Stan held her chair.

"My lady, ze chef prepared la boeuf ce soir."

He sat and faced her. He offered his hand so they could pray. So warm, so natural. Everything she wanted in life, she held in the palm of her hand. *Stan.*

His voice interrupted her thoughts. "Heavenly Father. We thank You for this bounty. Help the food strengthen our bodies. Thank you for bringing Nora into my life." His voice wavered a little. "Please bless her and her young ladies with every happiness they can ever imagine. Amen."

She squeezed his hand tightly. "And thank You for Stan," she inserted into the prayer, "and this wonderful friendship. Watch over him during his travels. Amen."

She released her grip, but somehow, during the meal, their hands joined together again. The rest of the meal was in silence, as it was when they washed the dishes. She had just given the counter one last wipe when she turned to find him watching her.

Stan cleared his throat. "Would you mind if I called occasionally?"

Nora shook her head. "Absolutely not. I want you to call every night, including weekends, if you don't mind." He smiled and nodded. "I hope you can call earlier some nights to talk to the girls. They adore you, you know?"

He sniffed before whispering, "I love them, too."

They didn't say much as they sat on the worn out sofa, gazed into each other's eyes and held hands. Finally at three in the morning, Stan stood.

"Look at the time. I've got to go."

"Not yet, please?"

"You need to get some sleep."

"You really think I'll be able to?"

He touched her nose. "Of course. When things get bad, just remember our friendship."

She started to lose it. The tears she had been holding back had built to flood level. One by one they crested her eyelids and fell to the floor.

"How will I be able to live without you being here for me or the girls?"

He wiped her tears. "We'll talk every night. It won't be so bad." Despite his words of comfort, she saw it, the pain in his eyes. "I have to get going. I've got an eight o'clock flight to catch."

Nora hugged him and whispered into his ear, "Please, don't go. Stay with me a little while longer. Stay until you have to leave." Her eyes pleaded as much as her words. In his eyes, she could see he was struggling.

In the end, he shook his head before giving her a final hug. "I really can't, my friend. But I'll never truly be gone. I'll always be here." When he pointed at her heart, it was too much. The dam of her strength failed. He held her tightly as she cried long and hard in his embrace.

***

Nothing had been this hard in his entire life, keeping up the façade. He couldn't take it anymore. Stan kissed her forehead and said goodbye. His own tears started before he reached the stairwell. They continued long after he reached his lonely apartment to pick up his bags.

Stan boarded his plane and departed for Los Angeles. At company headquarters, he spent the week in planning sessions. The future of the new company was on his shoulders so he dug in hard. The pain in his heart at having to say goodbye to 'his girls' gave him a reason to work even harder. The more he worked, the less he was reminded of all he'd left behind. And what he'd left behind was everything he'd ever wanted in life.

The night of the board meeting finally arrived. Much to Stan's surprise, Joe was right. The board discussed his appointment only briefly and then passed it unanimously on the first vote.

It was almost midnight when he called Nora. She answered on the first ring. "How'd it go?"

"First, tell me about your day and how the girls are."

As always, she described her day in detail, but spoke quickly. "Okay. I'm finished. Tell me how it went. What did the board say?"

"They approved it. I'm the new vice-president of research and development."

He was surprised her squeals didn't wake the girls. "I'm so proud of you. So, so proud of you. So what's next?"

"A little more planning, then off for a road trip."

"Sounds exciting. Gourmet meals, four-star hotels, chauffeurs, cocktails, in-flight movies."

"More like cold fries, lumpy mattresses, tiny rental cars and coach fare."

Her voice sobered. "I'm happy your dreams came true."

Her comment struck him at his core. *My greatest dream would have been to share life with you, as my wife.*

The road trip began two days later. The day between had been spent with Human Resources. When Stan was given the salary offer, his eyes popped. *Six* times higher than it had been, and his 'sign on' bonus would more than cover the cost of a brand new, very large home in Chicago. He had been financially on his own since before he graduated high school. But now, as long as he stayed employed with this company, he'd never have to worry about money. Joe told him his work ethic, creativity, organization and dedication had paid off. Stan's work future never looked brighter.

He left Los Angeles, flying into Buffalo. From Buffalo, he drove down to visit the R&D lab in Warren, Pennsylvania. The town was pretty and he got a good walk in before it turned dark. That night, he called Nora early so he could speak with the girls. They had missed him and Cassandra filled him in on school and the things her mom did at home.

But with Martina, it was different. "Can you come over, Stan?"

"I can't, honey, I'm hundreds of miles away."

"Come over. I want to play."

"I'd love that, but I can't."

"No! Come over, now."

Nora asked him to call back later. Martina was thoroughly upset.

Stan called after the children's bedtime. They talked for over an hour. Her voice was such a comfort and their friendship was so real, so deep. He could almost touch it. Not for the last time, he regretted not staying with Nora instead of leaving Sunday night.

In Warren, the reception Stan received was disheartening. It seemed the rumor was out that he was the new company's 'hatchet man'—that is, he was there to cut jobs, displace workers, ruin lives. Some of the lab employees tried to be overly nice and befriend him, but Stan saw through it right away. Others were downright nasty. That hurt Stan. He knew he was despised. *Is any amount of money worth this?*

He left the facility late, eating at an old bar in town. He couldn't wait to speak with Nora and tell her about his day. She'd understand. She would comfort him. And she did. That night set the pattern for almost the entire month of December, with one exception. Every site he visited, it was the same. Stan found his time on the road to be very lonely. But Nora was his comfort, his strength. While he may have been working and travelling, his reason to live was Nora and her girls.

The night of December sixteenth was very hard for Stan. That was the day when his divorce became final. At the lab in El Paso, everyone treated him like crap. He had problems concentrating. His mind kept drifting back to his relationship with Linda. Could he have done anything differently? What would have made her happy? Would it have been better to have never taken her home that snowy night in State College? Those thoughts were on his mind.

After stopping for dinner, he drove to a liquor store and bought a bottle of Johnny Walker Red. He planned on getting drunk after his call with Nora. Outside of the store, he sat staring at it. He needed something to help him through the night, but he knew he held a bomb in his hands. A bomb that had destroyed his father.

***

The girls wanted to talk to him, but he hadn't called yet when Nora tucked them in. He had missed the time he told her he would call. She was worried. The phone rang. Fear filled her heart. *Please, let it be him.* The fear left her when his voice came through the line.

"Hey, Nora."

"Stan, I was worried sick. Are you okay?"

"Actually, it was a pretty crappy day. I'm tired of being treated like a doormat."

"Want to talk about it?"

"No. All I really want is for you to tell me about your day. Tell me what the girls are up to. They excited for Santa to come?"

For the next fifteen minutes, she filled him in on what was happening in her world. He didn't ask the questions he normally did.

"That's it. Now, what about your day?"

"Not good."

"Why? What happened?"

A long hesitation. "I don't want to talk about it."

Her hair stood on end. Something was wrong. "What is it, Stan?"

"Just let it drop. I'll call you tomorrow and everything will be better, I promise."

The pit of her stomach tightened. What happened? It was more than just the job. Did he and Linda have a fight?

"You know you can talk to me about anything. I'm your best friend. You know that, right?"

His response was immediate. "Never been more sure of anything. Look, I just need a little me-time tonight. I'm gonna go now."

She was starting to shake inside. "Please don't go. Not like this."

"I need to go. Sorry about tonight. I... this ... it has nothing to do with you. It'll be better tomorrow. 'Night." He disconnected.

No, no. Two thoughts filled her mind. Either Stan and Linda were having serious problems or else Nora had done something to upset him. But he said it had nothing to do with her. It had to be something with Linda. He'd never acted like this. Something horrible must be going on. She needed to talk to him, now. In her heart, she knew Stan needed her.

"Wait, I have his itinerary," she mumbled to herself. She rustled through the papers he had given her. Nora's fingers were trembling. *Please, please, please have the number listed.*

There it was! She dialed, giving her number when the long distance operator came on. The hotel answered and rang his room. *Please answer, Stan.* But the phone just rang and rang and rang.

***

After the call, Stan opened the bottle of whiskey and poured a glass. He was staring at it when the phone started ringing. He ignored the call. Instead he lifted the glass. He stared at it for a very long time before taking that first sip. The brown liquid burned his tongue. He allowed it to swirl in his mouth. But he couldn't swallow.

This was exactly what had happened to his father. The downward spiral started with just one sip. Stan quickly walked to the sink and spit the alcohol out. Then he poured the remainder of the bottle down the drain. Despite this being the lowest moment in his life, he would not step over that threshold. His genes carried the traits of alcoholism, and nothing—no matter what—nothing was going to take him down that path. It had destroyed his childhood. He would not pass the unhappiness he'd suffered on to his children, if ever he had any.

Chapter 13

ora smiled. "It won't hurt to let the secret out of the bag now. Daddy didn't want any of you to know, especially you two, Cassie and Tina. He was afraid if you did, you might have thought less of your biological father. I never told any of you this, but we met long before you were born. We met in January of my senior year in high school. I was so attracted to Dad. He was kind, unlike anyone I'd ever known. He quickly became my best friend, my soulmate. We fell in love. But I was already engaged to Bob."

Nora drew a deep breath. Her daughters were looking at each other, as if in astonishment.

"I couldn't go back on my word. I told Dad I only wanted to be friends. He told me he wanted what was best for me. So Daddy disappeared from my life, completely. How I wanted him, how I needed him. If he had stayed, I never would have married Bob. I was that much in love with your father. But he was gone..."

The memories of losing her first husband came flooding back again. She closed her eyes and was once again next to Bob's hospital bed. Holding his hand when he drew his last breath and the monitors started alarming. Nora shook her head to drive the images away.

"Daddy finally came back into my life after Bob died. But it was after I'd already agreed to marry Tim. And once again, Daddy became my friend—my best friend— and my soulmate. I wanted him so badly, but he was married to Linda, or so he said."

They were interrupted by the sudden appearance of a doctor. The expression on his face chilled Nora to the bone.

***

In the early evening, the knock Nora had been waiting on came. Her heart was pounding out of her chest. Tim would arrive tomorrow morning, on Christmas Day, and would be there until New Year's. She had thought things through, planned and prayed about it. It was clear she knew what she wanted... no, *needed* to do.

Cassandra's squeal of delight brought her back to the present. Her daughter whipped open the door and wrapped her arms around Stan's legs. She was laughing with joy. Little Martina came running to hug him, but it was her words that brought tears to Nora's eyes.

Martina yelled excitedly, "Momma, Momma! Daddy's home!"

Stan swept both of her daughters in his arms. She couldn't help herself. She engulfed him in her hug. He pulled her head to his, his lips touching her ear.

"I missed you so much, Nora."

"Missed you, too. I knew you'd drop in. I have dinner ready. The girls have been looking forward to seeing you."

After dinner, Stan went out to his Blazer, bringing in their Christmas gifts. He couldn't be there on Christmas Day, so she allowed her daughters to open their gifts, just so he could see their faces. The little girls loved the things he'd purchased. Even the coat and boots he gifted to Nora were perfect.

All too soon, it was time for the girls' bath and bedtime ritual.

He stood to say goodbye, hugging the girls tightly. He turned to Nora.

She held his hands and whispered, "Come back in about an hour. I have something special for you."

He nodded. "I was going to ask if I could. I have something special for you, too."

***

It was almost eleven when he softly knocked on her door. Nora opened it immediately, giving him a very warm and firm hug. Stan had to pull away. "May I come in?"

Nora giggled. "Thought you'd never ask."

She held his hand as he entered the apartment. Two glasses of wine graced the table. He eyed her quizzically. "I see we're celebrating."

Nora couldn't help it. She snickered at him.

Her merriment was contagious. He joked, "You start early?"

Again, she giggled as she nodded her head. But behind the laughter, he caught a glimpse of sadness. Maybe she felt it, too. Tonight might be the last night he would ever see her. He wanted to tell her about his divorce. Wanted to beg her to forget Tim and choose him. After tonight, there was a distinct possibility happiness would be extinct to his soul, forever.

He kept it light. "So, is this your way of celebrating or did you need some help to have to put up with me?"

Her face turned serious as she touched his cheeks. "I've never put up with you. I've cherished every single moment we've spent together. I realized that this might be the last time we'll see each other for a while. I want to make it special, not just for me, but for you." She bit her lip and squeezed his hands.

"Nora, we'll manage to continue our friendship together, somehow. You are too important to me to just allow us to fade away. You don't know how badly I missed you these last couple of weeks. If we hadn't talked at night, I wouldn't have made it through that road trip."

She looked away. *Why?*

"I know exactly what you mean. I missed you so badly. It'll be different when you move to Chicago. And Tim will be here starting tomorrow for the next week, so we won't be able to talk. I mean, *talk as much*." She turned to meet his eyes.

His jaws clenched at the mention of Tim's name. He needed to tell her.

She must have seen it. She put a finger to his lips. "I have a proposal for you tonight and I really want it to happen."

He couldn't read her expression. "What proposal?"

"You're married to Linda and I'm engaged to Tim, but tonight, I don't want them to exist. Stan, I love you. I have since high school. I never told you..."

His heart fluttered and his soul leaped. His dreams were coming true!

Her eyes studied his. "I never told you how much you being in my life has meant to me. You are the best blessing of my life." Her eyes were suddenly wet. "When tomorrow dawns, our lives will be changed forever. But for tonight, you're my best friend. I don't ever want to wonder in the future what might have been. I need to know."

He was totally confused. "Nora, are you drunk?"

She looked at him with eyes that sparkled. "No, maybe a little tipsy, but not all of that's the wine. It's how I feel about you."

"But what about Tim? I mean..."

Her face darkened and she cut him off. "Tim doesn't exist tonight. Neither does Linda. I know you, Stanley, better than anyone. You love me, and as more than a friend, don't you?"

It was right there and he had trouble controlling his joy. "Yes, yes. So very, very much! And not just as a friend. But you're engaged..."

She put her fingers to his lips. "He doesn't exist tonight. The only two people in the world right now are you and me." She drew him close. "You don't know how long I've waited to do this." Slowly, Nora softly pressed her lips to his. The taste of her, the warmth of her body were too much. He lost control and kissed her back passionately and repeatedly. He reached for her hands. When they found the mark, their fingers laced together gently.

She pulled away. "Before we kiss again, I have a gift for you. I bought you something to remember me by." She walked over to the kitchen and removed a small box from the cupboard. She kissed his hand before handing it to him. "Open it."

"Just a second." He retrieved a small, six-inch long box from his coat pocket. "I got you something, too."

They smiled as they opened their gifts. Stan had bought her a beautiful bracelet of intertwined hearts. Half were silver and half were gold. He opened his gift to discover a handsome pocket watch. The inscription on the outside read: 'Stan, I've cherished each second you spent with me. Our love and friendship are timeless. Love, Nora.'

As he read the inscription, he had to bite his lips together. She told him to open it. When he did, he found a picture of Nora on the inside. He stared into her eyes and the look melted his heart.

She modeled her bracelet for him. "Thank you for the lovely bracelet. I'll cherish it forever." She reached up, laughed and brushed the hair from his eyes. "You need a haircut. You look like that guy from the sixties."

He laughed out loud. "Well, that narrows it down a little. Which guy are you talking about?"

"What's his name? He sang in a falsetto and had such long hair! Come on, Stan. You know... the one who sang that song about tiptoeing through the tulips."

"You mean Tiny Tim?" Stan's mouth dropped open. "I remind you of Tiny Tim?" She nodded and burst out in a guffaw. "You should patent that! A new form of birth control. Having the girl you love tell you that you remind her of Tiny Tim? What a way to ruin a moment of passion!"

Stan's face blushed as he realized what he had said.

Nora's eyes opened wide, matching her smile. "You really do love me? Not just saying that to make me feel good?"

Stan felt the heat on his cheeks. "No. I love you. Tried to hide it, but I didn't do a very good job, did I?" She shook her head slowly and grinned knowingly. "I wanted so much good to come into your life. Guess that's why I tried to help you out."

As he looked deeply into her eyes, he saw something he'd never seen before. His spirit soared thirty thousand feet above. *That look must certainly be love.*

Moment of truth. "I can't let this moment pass." He kissed her hand. "Nora, I have something important to tell you about Linda and me."

Her face suddenly lost all color. "Stop it. Don't make this worse than it's going to be."

"But I need to tell you this. I need to share with you."

Nora shook her head violently. "No, you don't. I don't care about her or what you want to tell me. Tomorrow, we'll pick up the pieces and hide it. We must, because there are others who would be destroyed by what is going on between us tonight. Tonight, there is no

Linda. There is no Tim. It's only you and me... unless you don't want me. I really hope you do. I've been dreaming about this for so long."

She quickly kissed him.

"I don't want to go through my life without knowing how it would be," she said, grasping his hand tightly. "I don't want that as a regret."

His spirit plummeted. He loved her, but she wasn't going to leave Tim. He understood her intentions now. When the sun rose in the morning, everything would be different, so much less than this moment. This would be the high point of their love and her happiness. Probably the pinnacle of his life. He wished their time together would never end, but tonight was all they had, forever. When the sun rose, his life would be over.

Stan's heart hurt. His love for Nora was eternal. He had loved her from the first moment he saw her years ago. If he had the chance, he'd make her and the girls happy beyond their wildest dreams. What he wanted to say was right on his lips, but she didn't want to hear it.

He studied her eyes. So beautiful. The same girl he first fell in love with. And she wouldn't stay with him because of Tim, the 'other' man. Tim, the lucky one. He must really be something special. Nora obviously loved him more that she loved Stan.

And tonight was it. Any chance for happiness would cease to exist in just a few short hours.

***

Nora kissed him again and whispered, "Tonight, let's pretend you and I are together, forever. Man and wife. Living out our dreams in a fairy tale that never ends. I want to make love with my best friend." His eyes were so deep, so handsome. "Will you make love with me?"

He started to pull away. "We don't have to do this. I can see the love on your face. That's enough..."

"I want this, Stan. Please, don't make me beg. Do you want me?"

His eyes clouded. "You know I do. I want you so badly I can taste it. But please, not just for one night."

I won't let you give up your happiness for me. "This is all there can be. Make love with me."

His hands were shaking where he touched her. "I love you. From the moment I first saw you. Always have, always will."

She smiled, leading him back to the bedroom. It felt so natural to hold his hand. She walked to her dresser and turned Tim's photo down so she couldn't see his face. She removed her engagement ring. She caught Stan watching her in the mirror.

"We don't have to do this. I can feel..."

Nora turned, bolstering her courage with a smile. "I wouldn't miss this for the world." She kissed him again, then closed the door.

***

Stan watched Nora sleep. She was the most beautiful woman he'd ever seen. What they'd just shared was like nothing he'd ever dreamed was possible. Their connection was perfect. The real joy hadn't been physical. Instead it was in his heart and soul.

He glanced at the clock, almost five. The girls would be getting up soon. He still had the gifts from 'Santa' in the Blazer. He kissed Nora's hair, lingering for a second to breathe in her delectable scent. He dressed, quickly running outside to retrieve the bag of gifts. After he'd placed them under the tree, he took a bite out of a cookie and drank some of the milk the girls had set out for Santa. Stan sobbed and almost choked on the milk. He wouldn't be here to see the girls open up their gifts.

Stan returned to watch Nora sleep for a few more moments. But when he heard Martina's voice, asking

Cassandra if she was awake, Stan knew it was time to go. He kissed Nora a final time and whispered, "I love you and always will. I... I... goodbye... *my love.*"

Stan quietly left, locking her apartment door. He fought to maintain his composure. Christmas Day was the worst of his life. He wracked his mind trying to figure a way to win Nora's heart and bring them together. By noon, his head throbbed horribly and he had no idea what he could do. How could he live without her? He didn't have a clue.

***

In her bed, Nora hadn't been sleeping, only pretending. Not for herself, but for Linda. She hoped the witch appreciated it. Nora knew that if she had spoken, she would've begged him to leave his wife. Nora would never let this man go. She would offer Stan all she had, her body, her soul, her undying love forever and ever, for right or for wrong. But it was over.

Nora held back her tears until she heard the apartment door close. *God, I can't take the pain. Take me home, please.* Not even losing Bob had hurt like this. She wanted, no, needed him. It had nothing to do with the money. She couldn't have cared less if they lived in poverty, as long as they were together. The love they had was so right, but apparently so wrong. She cursed her life, asking God why she and Stan couldn't be together.

The reality of life as a single parent surfaced when her girls knocked on her door. Cassandra whispered excitedly, "Mommy, come look! Santa came."

Santa? I couldn't afford to get anything from Santa.

She hugged her daughters. "There's something I need to tell you about Santa. We moved since last year and I forgot to mail Santa to tell him our new address. He didn't know where we lived and couldn't bring anything this year."

Cassandra laughed as she handed her mother a wrapped gift she hadn't seen before. "Look, Momma! You were wrong. He *did* know where we live!"

As Nora stared in disbelief, Martina and Cassandra tore the wrappings off their presents. Santa had brought them the Cabbage Patch dolls both of them so desperately wanted.

Stan. He'd done it again. And he wasn't even here to see this. He had brought such magic to her daughters. She knew he must've gotten them to tell him what they had asked Santa for. And he came through, just as he always did.

"Momma," Martina asked, "are you gonna open your gift from Santa?"

Cassandra pulled out another present from under the tree. "Look, Mommy! There are two gifts for you! Santa must think you were a very good girl!"

Nora quickly wiped her cheeks and forced a smile. "He brought two presents for me?" She couldn't believe Santa had brought her a gift. Both girls stood next to her as she opened the packages. First, she opened the bigger one, revealing a purse. Her heart swelled with love for Stan's thoughtfulness. It was exactly the style she wanted.

Cassandra handed her the second package. Slowly, Nora ripped the paper off and gasped. It was a new 35-millimeter camera. Also inside the box were several rolls of film and a flash attachment. Then she noticed a small piece of paper at the bottom.

Dear Nora,

Ho-Ho-Ho. Life is full of memories. Please take the time to capture them so someday when they're starting to fade, you can look back and relive each precious moment. Someone told me that photography was once your hobby. You were very good at it and enjoyed it, once upon a time. Santa didn't have room under the tree for the tripod, camera case or the other things that go with your present. The reindeer put them in your Tahoe. Enjoy them. Merry Christmas!

Love, Santa

She'd never told Stan she wanted a camera. How had he known? Apparently he remembered when she'd shared her photo album with him in high school. *He really is my soulmate.* Her heart was about to break into a million pieces.

She was just going through the motions as she prepared breakfast for the girls.

Martina asked, "What time will Stan come?"

"He can't come over today."

"Why?"

"Because he's busy."

"Why?"

"He has to unpack from his trip."

"Why?"

"Don't keep asking me 'why'?"

"Okay. Why are you crying?"

"I'm not crying. It's... it's... allergies."

After breakfast, the girls gave her the gifts Stan had bought in their names. This was too much. *I don't care.* She tried to call Stan. She'd made up her mind. She would tell him that last night couldn't be it. She no longer cared that he was married to Linda. She wanted a life with him and she would tell him so. But Stan didn't answer her call. The line just rang busy.

She decided she would pack the girls up and take them to his apartment, but didn't even know where he lived. *Please send him over.* The thought entered her mind like a rock dropping from an airplane. She *did* know where he lived! His address was on the car registration!

"Girls. Get your coats."

A loud knock sounded on her door. Was God answering her prayer? Was it Stan?

Martina must have thought so. "Momma, Daddy's home!" But when her daughter opened the door, it wasn't Stan.

It was Tim.

Chapter 14

*T*he news was going to be bad. Nora felt it. So did her family. Fear choked her. Her eyes touched on her daughters. Martina—the staunch lawyer who never showed emotion—covered her mouth with her hand. Cassandra reached for Martina's arm and they clung to each other. Kaitlin, happy go lucky Kaitlin, was trying to be strong, but her face gave it away. Kelly couldn't even look at the doctor. Jeremy and Geeter now stood at Nora's sides, bracketing her.

Dignified despite the fear in her heart, Nora asked, "Did my husband die?"

The doctor glanced at all of them before responding, "Mrs. Jenkins, your husband's heart is very weak. Honestly, I don't know how long he'll be with us. The trauma of the heart attack, prolonged CPR and defibrillation took a lot out of him. I hope I'm wrong, I really do. But, if you have anything in your soul you want to say to him, now might be your last chance. We moved him to cardiac ICU. Let me walk you in."

Nora was too traumatized to say anything. Only three visitors could enter at one time. Kaitlin and Martina volunteered. The three women followed the doctor and exited the elevator at the fifth floor. They passed through secured doors to a highly monitored care unit. Soon they were by Stan's bed. Tubes and wires from I.V. bags and monitors were attached to him. His skin color was very pale. The doctor left. Nora reached for Stan's hand.

Nora was empty inside. She remembered holding the hand of her first husband as he'd drawn his last breath. Somehow she'd survived, probably because she knew her two little girls couldn't live without her. But now, the man she loved more than life itself—her true soulmate—was in a hospital bed. This might very well be the last bed he'd ever be in. She'd survived Bob's death, but she knew she couldn't survive Stan's passing.

She leaned over to kiss his forehead. Into his ear, she whispered, "Stan, I loved you since that first day we met in school. My only regret is that I didn't spend every second of my life from that day forward with you by my side. Don't leave me, sweetheart. I can't live without you. Please don't leave me."

Her thoughts were interrupted when his monitors suddenly started a loud annoying chirping. Nora looked at the flashing values on the screen. *Oh no. If You are taking him, take me, too!* She clung tightly to Stan's hand as the room suddenly filled with nurses. Someone started screaming, "He's coding! Get the crash cart!"

The nurses pushed Nora out of the way, a little too hard. She lost her balance, falling backwards toward the hard tile floor.

***

Tim walked in, grabbed Nora and kissed her lips. He reached for Martina. "Yes, sweetheart, Daddy's home!" He looked confused when Martina broke out in tears and ran from the room. Looking at Nora, his expression drooped. "Well, that certainly wasn't the reception I hoped for."

Nora wiped the tears from her eyes. Her thoughts were on Stan instead of Tim, but she put on a good front. "Hi. It's good to see you. Merry Christmas."

"I missed you, Nora." He held up a shopping bag, shaking it. "Guess what? Santa brought presents! Call the girls back in."

Nora nodded and walked into the girls' room, talking quietly so Tim wouldn't hear. "Girls, Stan is gone. Tim is here. He's going to be your daddy."

Martina placed her hands on her hips and defiantly answered, "No! Not my Daddy!"

Nora dropped to her knees and hugged her. "Please don't sass Mommy. Please do as I say, okay?" Neither of her daughters looked happy.

As they walked back to the tree, Tim was staring at all the gifts the girls and Nora had unwrapped earlier. He looked at Nora with confusion. "Thought things were so tough. Looks like you had a great Christmas. Tips must have been really good." He held up Nora's new winter coat. "Where'd you get this?"

"I picked it out," Cassandra answered before Nora could say a word, "and Stan bought it for Mommy."

Tim's eyes shifted from Cassandra to Nora. "Stan? Who's Stan?"

Defiantly, Martina placed her hands on her hips and let the goose out of the bag. "Stan's my daddy."

"Your what? Did you say 'your daddy'?" His face was filled with anger, but he calmed himself before speaking again. "Nora, explain who Stan is."

For the next hour, Nora told Tim an abbreviated tale of how he was an old friend who had come into their life for a while and helped them out, but now was gone for good. The tension between them was like a tripwire attached to a bomb. One wrong move and everything would blow up.

167

It didn't help when the girls opened Tim's gifts—some off-brand doll supposed to resemble a Barbie. They threw them down and played with their Cabbage Patch dolls.

After the girls went to bed, Tim asked Nora to sit with him on the couch. "I know you didn't tell me the truth."

That's an understatement. "What do you mean?" she asked.

"Come on, Nora. Something's happened here. It's plain to see while I was off earning enough for us to get married, someone else was filling my shoes. Did he fill my bed, too?"

Nora's guilt overwhelmed her. She couldn't lie any more than she could look in his eyes. "Yes, I slept with him. I'm sorry. It... it just happened, but now it's over, for good."

She thought he would explode at her, but instead, he softly stroked her hair. "That's okay. I shouldn't have left you alone like I did. Was it just one last fling before we get married? Or was it more? Please tell me you were just seeding your last wild oats."

His eyes were full of understanding when she finally looked into them.

"If it was just a fling, that's okay," he added. He looked away and his face turned red. "I sowed my own wild oats during this trip, too. It was wrong, but I wanted one last shot at Laney before you and I walked down the aisle. I took her to Europe with me. I know I shouldn't have done that, but I needed to see what she meant to me. By the third week, I knew I didn't really want her."

Nora was shell shocked.

"I wanted to close the door with Laney before you and I got married," Tim's voice continued, though Nora could barely take it in. "She's in the past now. If you forgive me, then I'll forgive you... unless this is something more... Something here I need to worry about?"

Nora was fuming. "So while I struggled to feed the girls, you traveled across Europe with your ex-girlfriend?"

He laughed. "At least I didn't commit adultery, like you did. That's against the law in most states."

Nora was sick to her stomach. She was angry he'd cheated on her, but then, she'd cheated, too. She was no better than Tim. Her mind drifted to Stan. She wanted him so badly, but he was married to Linda. That hadn't changed. She really didn't have a choice, did she?

Nora sadly shook her head and replied, "No, Tim. It's all in the past. That door is closed for me, too."

Tim smiled, kissing her lips softly. "Nora, I don't want to wait any longer to get married. I looked at my schedule and the first Saturday in January will be our wedding day."

Inside, she cringed. *More like a death sentence.* She didn't love Tim and really doubted she ever would. *I wish I was marrying Stan.* That was one wish that would never come true. The marriage to Tim was only for the benefit of her girls. Tim would be a good provider for them, she hoped. She forced a smile. "Let me see if my mom can make it, okay?"

"I already booked the church. She'll just have to make it." An odd smile spread across his face. "Now, I've been thinking about you all day. Let's go get reacquainted."

Nora's soul was empty as he led her by the hand to her bedroom. Less than five minutes later, he turned from her and started to snore.

He treated me like a whore. As Nora lay in bed, she remembered Stan's touch. Every move he had made was to please her. In fact, he had *pleased* her more in a couple of hours than Bob had during their entire marriage. And afterwards, the way Stan had cuddled with her made her feel so loved.

She stared at the ceiling. *This is how my life will be from now on.* Suddenly, the urge to vomit hit her. She barely made it to the bathroom before her stomach emptied. Afterwards, she took a shower, scrubbing away every trace of Tim.

***

Stan was finished packing by five on Christmas day. His telephone had been the first thing to go in a box, simply to avoid the temptation of calling Nora and begging her to leave Tim for him. His suitcase contained enough clothes for a week. He'd return later to retrieve the rest of his things. As he surveyed the boxes, he was surprised how damned little he had in the way of material things. He'd spent more money on Nora and the girls for Christmas than the value of all his belongings put together.

He was on the road by six, driving from Detroit to Chicago. He spent the night at a motel. Early the next morning, Stan met with a realtor. For the next two days, they toured house after house. Stan thought he would know it when he saw the right property. It happened to be a sprawling Colonial in the middle of a block of homes in a development called Oak Lawn.

The house was immaculate. It had a large maple out front. Sadly, Stan could picture a tire swing he and Nora would use to swing their girls on. *I need to stop this.* He shook off the thought.

The realtor explained, "It was the model home for this development. For the past two years, the house was the sales office for the developer. It comes fully furnished. The developer moved out this week and so it just came on the market yesterday." The realtor told him the asking price, which was very reasonable.

After a brief tour, Stan turned to the realtor and said, "I'll take it."

The man was all smiles as he sat Stan down at the kitchen table, opening his briefcase. "So let's talk about the minimum down payment and what your monthly mortgage will look like. First, I need to know your annual salary."

Stan gazed around at the kitchen, but all he could see was him and Nora cooking dinner together for their little girls. He cleared his throat before turning to the realtor. "I make more in a year than your entire agency pulls in. There'll be no down payment." Stan pulled his checkbook from his pocket and wrote out a check for the full amount. "I know there are closing costs and such, but here's the payment for the house itself. My only stipulation is I want to move in tomorrow, as soon as the check clears. I'll stay here and pay rent, if required, until we close on the rest of the deal."

The realtor gave him a strange look. "Uh, that's not the way it's done. I'm not sure we can do that."

Stan took his check back from the realtor's hand, ripping it in two. "Okay, you're fired. I'll find another realtor who'll do what I want. This will be my house." Stan stood and started to walk to the door.

The look on the realtor's face was pure fear. Stan could read his mind. He had a live one, ready to pay full asking price, but he was getting away. "Mr. Jenkins, give me a few minutes. I'll call the office and see what we can do."

Stan held up his checkbook. "You're on the clock. Every ten minutes of delay, my offer goes down one thousand dollars."

The realtor sped off in search of a pay phone. He was back in less than five minutes, telling Stan that the seller agreed to the deal. Stan wrote out a second check.

At ten the next morning, he received a call from the realtor, letting him know his check had cleared. Stopping by the office, Stan picked up the keys. He kept himself busy that week, having the locks rekeyed, getting utilities transferred to his name and cleaning. He purchased a new mattress and sheets for the king-sized bed in the master bedroom because when he pulled back the covers to get ready for washing, he found evidence someone had been using the bed for a distinctly non-business purpose.

He also purchased all new appliances. The house was gigantic with lots and lots of space. Behind the garage was a large room for a workshop. Stan always wanted one, so he went to Sears, treating himself by buying a complete set of tools.

Stan toiled from early in the morning until late at night, but all he could think about were his three girls. He found himself talking to her. "I wish you could see this place, Nora. Big backyard for the girls to play in. You and I, we'd put up two swings so they wouldn't have to go to the park."

The hole in his heart was so big. "This place is like a palace, but it's just not a home without you. I'd give anything just to have one more day with you." He pulled the watch she'd given him from his pocket. It was the only picture he had of her. He gently touched it to his lips. "Love you so much." He spent New Year's Eve listening to the Muppet tape and reminiscing.

The week had been a long and emotional one for Stan. He had the house of his dreams, but it just wasn't a home. He was so lonely because there was no one to share it with. Oh, there was someone he *wanted* to share it with, but she belonged to someone else.

He missed Nora. Missed the sound of her voice, the way her eyes sparkled when they talked. He knew it had been wrong for them to make love, but that Christmas Eve night was the one day in his life he would cherish forever. He'd never be that happy again, ever. Of that he was sure.

Nora had told him Tim would be leaving on New Year's Day, so he waited until January second to call her. He needed to hear her voice. He wanted to see how she was doing, to tell her about the house and give her his new phone number. He dialed her apartment in the late afternoon. His call was answered on the second ring.

"Hello," a man's voice said.

Stan thought he had dialed incorrectly. "Oh, I'm sorry. I must have the wrong number."

"Maybe, but I don't think so. Were you trying to reach Nora?"

A bad feeling started to climb up Stan's spine. "Yes, I was trying to reach Nora Crittendale. I dialed the wrong number, didn't I?"

"No, you dialed correctly, Stan. I'm Tim. I knew you'd call. That's why I hung around. And I know what you want with my fiancée."

Stan stuttered, "I, uh, I j-j-just wanted to w-w-wish her a Happy New Year."

"I bet you did. Let's be honest, okay? You just wanted to do her again, didn't you?"

Stan didn't say a thing.

"Thought so," the voice snorted. "Well, those days are over, buddy. Nora and I are getting married this Saturday, so don't you dare bother her again. And I mean like, ever again. She told me how you tricked her into sleeping with you, you bastard. You'll never have her again. She's mine, get it? Do I make myself perfectly clear?"

Now what do I do? Before he could say a word, Nora's voice echoed in the background. "Tim, who are you talking to?"

"I'm talking to Stan. Remember him? He's the guy you slept with. I told him never to contact you again!"

"You have no right to say those things. Hand me the telephone."

"Like hell. I don't want him talking to you, ever." Tim then turned his conversation back to Stan. "You heard me, didn't you, Stan?"

"Yes, I did." Stan started to hang up.

"If you ever call her again, you mother..."

Stan disconnected the call.

Not only had he not been planning on ever talking to Tim, he'd gotten Nora in trouble. He shook his head. "That's it. I need to leave her alone. It's over, for good," he muttered, struggling to maintain control. The best part of his life was over.

Out loud he ranted, "God, why did it have to be this way? I finally found Nora again and I screwed it up! Why didn't I tell her I was divorced and beg her to leave Tim and marry me? I should have told her I was in love with her? I wish I were dead!"

***

Nora was seething.

"How dare you use that kind of language in front of the girls. Do that again and I'll, I'll—"

"You'll what? Leave me for him? He's married, you forget that? He used you to cheat on his wife." He stood and kicked over the chair. "I'm going out. You think about what you want to be... my wife... or some pitiful whore who sleeps with married men."

Tim stormed out, but not before slamming the door.

He returned late in the evening, drunk as a skunk. She'd had the whole day to think about the situation. Tim was right. She did have a decision to make—marry Tim or not? *I don't have a choice.* The marriage was a way to provide for her girls. They came first.

The girls were in bed when he got back. He could barely stand.

"Make your mind up?"

Nora couldn't answer. She simply nodded.

"Good. I'll let you make it up to me." He grabbed her arm and yanked her to the bedroom.

***

Stan started his new job the next day. He was numb after his call to Nora's apartment. He'd only wanted to talk to her, not cause a problem between her and her fiancé. He'd never call her again. *It's over. I lost her, again.* He worked late the next couple of days. His last ties to Detroit were in his apartment. Stan rented a U-Haul to complete the move to Chicago.

His mind drifted. Nora's face appeared before him. *Stop it.* He'd never contact her again. Broken heart or not, it wasn't worth the risk of causing her further pain.

***

In Detroit, Nora watched in disbelief as Tim packed their belongings, throwing out the things he felt they didn't need. She was too numb to even argue about it. They would move to Cleveland on Sunday, the day after their wedding. *No, not our wedding... his wedding.*

Thursday would be her last day at the restaurant. She worked dayshift on Wednesday. It was a slow day and Nora had time to write a goodbye letter to Stan. Tears filled her eyes as she kissed the envelope before sealing it.

"I have no idea how to get this to you," she whispered to herself. A quiet voice softly resonated in her ears. *"You know where he works. Get it there."*

Stan had told her about his office. She remembered his secretary's name was Gwen. *I need to do this now before I lose my nerve.* Her fingers trembled as she searched the phone book for the number. When the receptionist answered, she asked for Gwen.

A few seconds passed. "Gwen Lupinski, may I help you?"

"Uh, Gwen. I know you won't remember me, but I'm Nora Crittendale."

Gwen's voice was pleasant. "I do remember you. Mr. Jenkins always spoke kindly about you. How are you?"

"I... I'm okay. I know Stan, I mean Mr. Jenkins, is transferring to Chicago. Did he move yet?"

"Yes and no. He's working in Chicago, but I'm not sure he took everything yet. He still has a few things here in his office. I believe he told me he'd pick them up within the month. Why do you ask?"

"I, uh, have something I want to get to him. Do you have an address for him?"

"I'm not sure. I could check with Human Resources to see if they have it for his place in Chicago. However, there's another alternative. If you drop it off here, I'll personally make sure he gets it."

Thank God she had listened to that small, quiet voice. If Nora didn't do it right now, she might not ever get the chance. She was scared Tim might find out she left to run the letter over, but it didn't matter.

She told Gwen, "I'll be there in a few minutes."

Chapter 15

*N*ora's body slammed against the tile floor. When she lost her balance, Kaitlin and Martina had reached for her. But they missed. The misery shooting from Nora's hip was eclipsed by extremely intense pain across her chest. The world around her dimmed, even as her two darling daughters tried to help her up. It felt like she was falling again, but she was already on the floor.

Suddenly, she was at the top of the room. The nurses used a defibrillator to shock Stan's body once, twice and a third time. They seemed to stop and breathe a sigh of relief. Then they turned toward Nora. To Nora's surprise, they suddenly pushed her daughters out of the way and started CPR on her—well... not her... but on her body.

The entire scene was amazing.

A very familiar voice interrupted her thoughts, "You'd think the things they're doing to your body would hurt, but I didn't feel a thing. Can you feel them working on you?"

Nora turned quickly to see Stan smiling at her. She leapt into his arms, now feeling complete. Euphoria filled her heart.

Stan laughed. "Admit it. You just couldn't get enough of me, could you?"

She shook her head and clung tightly to him. Stan kissed her lips before gently pushing Nora away to arm's length. "I love you, Nora. I actually loved you the day I first saw you. And just like you, my biggest regret is that I didn't spend every second of my life with you after we first met."

They embraced once again. Slowly, they pulled away to look into each other's eyes. Stan's face clouded before he smiled at her. "I'm going back, Nora. Please come back with me. I don't think it's our time to die, not yet. I need you, I want you, I love you. Please come back with me. I love you, eternally." The vision of Stan slowly disappeared from her view.

Suddenly Nora was back in her body. The pain in her chest was excruciating. She didn't care and she smiled at her girls just before her world turned black.

***

Stan was having trouble sleeping. All he could think about was Nora and the lost opportunity for happiness. It was midnight. Sleep wasn't coming. If he couldn't sleep, he might as well get on the road. Stan saddled up, pointing his mini-Blazer east for the six-hour drive to Detroit.

Slick roads fifty miles out of Chicago made the commute longer than he had planned. But by eight in the morning, he had picked up the U-Haul and parked it in front of his old apartment. It took him all of thirty minutes to get everything loaded. He had two more things to do before he left Detroit. He needed to stop by the office and say goodbye to a few people. Then, he planned to stop at his Tahoe to drop off the key to Nora's apartment, along with the goodbye letter he'd written. He had four other things he wanted to give her.

Gwen Lupinski had been his secretary. As a farewell gift, Stan had picked up an inspirational book written by

Billy Graham for her, as well as a small bouquet of flowers. He arrived at the plant a little after nine. He walked around, shook everyone's hands and said goodbye. He looked for Gwen as well, but someone told him she was going to be late coming in. He decided he'd call her later.

His last box of personal belongings was packed in the Blazer. As he glanced at his old office one last time, he realized he still had his access badge. He walked back inside to turn it in to Human Resources. As he exited the front door, he almost ran into Gwen.

"Mr. Jenkins! I didn't know you were coming in today."

He smiled at her. "Glad I saw you before I left. There's a little something at your desk. I just wanted to take a moment to tell you how much I enjoyed working with you. It's been such an honor. If there is anything, anything at all I can do for you in the future, let me know."

She shot him a sad smile. "It was also a pleasure working with you, Mr. Jenkins. And the same goes for me, too. If you need anything, you know where I'll be."

"Gwen, I want you to think about coming to work for me in Chicago. If that is something you and your husband would consider, please let me know. The offer isn't just for now, but for anytime you want it. Goodbye." He hugged her before walking to his vehicle. He started the engine and was just about to shift it into gear when he heard a knock at his window. It was Gwen.

She looked relieved. "Mr. Jenkins? Thank God you didn't leave. I almost forgot something. Mrs. Crittendale dropped off an envelope for you two days ago. I promised I'd get it to you. Would you walk in with me? It's locked in my desk."

The world started spinning. He forced himself to breathe naturally. Stan shut down the Chevy and walked back into the building with her. He watched Gwen unlock her center drawer before removing the envelope. She handed it to him, but as he grasped it, she didn't let go.

She caught his eye. "If I may be so bold, I'd suggest you read whatever is inside very carefully and very soon. It must have been important to Nora... I mean... Mrs. Crittendale. When she gave it to me, she broke down crying, asking me... no... begging me to watch over you. She was quite upset. It took me a half hour to get her to stop crying. I don't know what's happening between the two of you. None of my business, but whatever it is, I really hope it works out, for both your sakes." She reached up and kissed his cheek before saying goodbye.

In the parking lot, Stan climbed into the Blazer. Nora's fragrance filled his being. He ripped the letter open.

Dearest Stan, my best friend, my soulmate, my love.

I wanted to apologize for the horrible way Tim treated you when you called the other day. I so longed to hear your voice one more time, to tell you again how much I love you. I hope you know I always will. I was a fool on Christmas Eve, not for allowing what happened to happen, but for letting you go. I did it because you were married. I regret that decision now.

It doesn't matter to me anymore. You are the love of my life. I was so stupid to let you go. I had you, sweetheart, in my hands, but let you slip through my fingers. I pretended to be asleep just before you left. You don't know how hard it was to lie still in that bed when you told me you were leaving, and not jump into your arms.

You and I were meant to be together, no one can deny that. But somehow we didn't end up that way, did we? Life is cruel and it sucks, for both of us. Until the day I die, I will regret losing you not only once, but twice.

On Christmas Eve, I should have held you, confessed my undying love for you and made you understand that any chance for happiness in my life went with you that night. The sound of the door closing behind you broke my heart into a million pieces. My heart will never be whole again without you. But that will never happen, so for you, I hope you and Linda find the happiness I wish was ours. I will love you forever, Stanley!

Goodbye, my love, goodbye!

Stan had trouble seeing after he put down the letter. His mind ran in every direction imaginable. Was it too late? He ripped up the goodbye note he'd written her. He no longer needed it. There was still time to make this right, still time for hope.

It was crystal clear. He knew exactly what he had to do, but time was running out. He planned on changing the future, and by God, he would do it or die trying.

***

Clara Thomas, Nora's mother, sat on a kitchen chair watching *her* little girl prepare for the wedding rehearsal. *Unbelievable.* Nora's heart wasn't in to marrying Tim. She was providing for the girls. Clara had tried to talk some sense into her, but Nora was determined. Her stubborn daughter was more interested in making sure the girls were taken care of than in her own happiness.

Wish there was some way to help. It had taken most of her Social Security income for the entire month just to make it to this so called sham of a wedding. Tim didn't want a wife, he wanted a servant to take care of him and satisfy his physical needs.

The drive to the church was very quiet. Tim abused Stan's Tahoe, hitting every pot hole he could find. He told Nora that as soon as they were married, he was going to buy a new Tahoe for himself. He'd give her his old K-car.

At the church, Tim introduced Nora and Clara to Pastor Jim, who would be performing the marriage service the following day. Tim's family had arrived from St. Louis earlier and were waiting at the church. His brothers would be the groomsmen. His sister-in-laws would be the bridesmaids. Tim informed Nora he had picked out his own sister as the Maid of Honor. *What the...?* Didn't he have any consideration for Nora at all? Clara shook her head silently, asking God to intervene before the train wreck occurred.

Clara studied her daughter's eyes. They were vacant. Nora clearly wanted the wedding to be over as soon as possible. Anyone could see this wasn't Nora's wedding at all. It was Tim's. Her daughter was only a participant— no, a victim. His every word and action made it plain this was his show. Tim had stated time and again since he had to pay for everything, it would be just like he wanted it to be. Nora was heading toward her fate (or more likely, doom) as Tim bossed everyone around, especially her daughter. Twice, he yelled at her in front of everyone, humiliating her. He certainly did love to be in control.

In the first row, Clara held Cassandra and Martina as she watched the farce unfold. She wished her husband was still living. He would have stopped this disaster. He would have stood up to this bully and made everything right. Were there no good men left in this world?

The sound of a door closing caught her attention. She turned and noticed a tall man standing at the rear of the church, watching, observing. When Tim screamed at Nora again, that man's face showed pain.

She turned to watch Nora cringe. *God, this has to be horrible for her.* From her body language, Clara could tell

Nora wasn't happy at all. No, this wasn't just horrible. It was torture. She was a lamb being led to slaughter with no hope of rescue. Clara prayed for a miracle.

Pastor Jim's voice filled the church. "As soon as the two of you repeat your vows, I'll ask the congregation if there is anyone who objects to the wedding. To speak now or forever hold their peace. No one ever does, you know." The minister laughed.

A clear voice erupted from the back of the church. "And what happens if someone does object?" The man slowly walked toward the altar. "What if there is someone who doesn't 'forever hold his peace'?"

Every head in the sanctuary turned, straining to see whose booming voice had spoken those words.

Cassandra and Martina wriggled from her grip. They recognized the voice and streaked down the aisle.

Martina screamed, "Daddy! Daddy!" and both girls leapt into his arms, hugging him tightly.

Clara turned in disbelief to stare at Nora, but the look on Tim's face caught her attention first. It was plain to see he also knew that voice.

Tim rolled up his sleeves while walking toward Stan. "You bastard! You *will* pay for this intrusion into my wedding rehearsal!"

Nora apparently understood who spoke those words, too. For the first time all night, color seeped back into her face. Her eyes had life in them and they were wide open.

The man continued walking toward the altar, now with Nora's daughters in his arms. His bold voice was directed to the pastor. "What if there is someone who objects strongly to Nora spending her life with a guy who will never make her happy? Someone who loves only himself? Someone she obviously doesn't really love?"

The man was now abreast of Tim, but ignored him. "What happens if someone comes along who really loves her, who cares more about her happiness than his own?

What should he do, Pastor? How do we go about this, because I object to this travesty? As God is my witness, I will not allow this to happen!"

Tim growled, "Put down the girls and I'll show you how it goes." Tim's brothers had joined Tim and surrounded him on three sides.

Can this be happening? Clara's body trembled with hope. She turned to her daughter. "Is this the man you told me about? Is this your friend Stan?"

Nora had tears in her eyes as she nodded. It was the first time she had smiled all day.

Tim barked, "Yes, this is Stan. He's the jerk who just interrupted my wedding rehearsal. The one I warned to leave Nora alone. And he's about to leave, either on his own or with my foot shoved up his ass! Now put the girls down and leave before I kick you to kingdom come!"

Clara turned to the man who held her granddaughters. Hope was building in her heart. "Why are you here, Stan? State your intentions and be quick about it!"

Stan smiled at her. "Good evening, Mrs. Thomas. I'm sorry we have to meet like this. I recognized you from the picture in the girls' room. Actually, I recognized you from the picture that used to hang in your home when we were teenagers. You haven't changed. As lovely as ever. But that's not what you wanted to know."

He kissed both girls' foreheads.

"You asked me a question," Stan said. "Why am I here? Mrs. Thomas, I came here tonight to keep your daughter from making the biggest mistake of her life. You see, I love Nora, very much. I came to tell her that and to ask if... no... to *beg* her to be my wife."

Wait. This wasn't making sense. "Nora told me you're married. How can you ask her to be your wife if you're already married?"

Stan laughed a joyous and crystal clear laugh that filled the sanctuary. He ignored everyone else. His eyes were on Nora.

"Mrs. Thomas, I'm no longer married to anyone! My divorce became final nine days before Christmas. I'm a single man."

***

Nora shuddered. "What? You divorced Linda and didn't think to tell me about it?"

Stan still held Nora's two daughters tightly in his arms. "No, I tried to tell you twice, but you didn't want to hear it. Afterwards, I couldn't tell you. You told me you were happy and I tried to respect that. But after what I've seen tonight, I know that wasn't true."

Anger was building inside her. She had to struggle to get her breath. "Then you should have kept trying! Why didn't you? Why couldn't you tell me the truth?"

Stan smiled at her. "You told me you were happy. After what we did, I was afraid to tell you about the divorce. I was afraid you'd feel guilty or obligated to be with me, not out of love, but because you would be afraid of hurting me. I worried that by being with me, you might walk away from what truly made you happy. But as I watched this farce tonight, I know the truth."

Her heart was breaking. Stan had betrayed her. "Were you too dumb to realize what was happening... what I was telling you by my actions? And on Christmas morning, you just walked away from me? You had to know how badly I wanted you, to have a life with you. Even if I didn't say so, as my best friend, you must have felt it."

Nora struggled to restrain the overwhelming urge to slap him. "And it was all right there. The obstacle I feared most, your marriage to Linda, was over. Happiness was within our reach but you led me to believe you were still married to her. You used me, just like Tim uses me! You took what you wanted and left. So remember this, Stanley, it wasn't me that ruined our chance for happiness. You are the one who let everything slip through your fingers. You screwed up and ended us before we could even begin. This is all your fault. You lied to me, Stanley."

Nora noted his expression had changed. His smile was gone, only to be replaced by the look of dread. "I only lied to protect you."

How dare you. "To protect me? No, you lied to take advantage of me. Took everything I had to offer and walked away. Then you stand there and say you lied to protect me? Bullshit! Put my girls down, now."

Stan did as he was told. Nora walked up to him and slapped him as hard as she could. "That is for being a bastard! Early on, I told you I couldn't stand you lying to me, yet you did. You lied to me again! Do you understand that? You knew how I felt. You knew what I wanted and what did you do?"

She had to stop for a second to catch her breath.

"You lied and left me there to suffer all alone when you walked away." She slapped him a second time, his cheek already bright red from her hand. "And that slap was for lying to me."

His face was contorted. "But you lied, too. You told me you were happy." He turned and swept his hand toward Tim. "I watched you here tonight. That was crap. You know I'm the only one who can make you happy. I am the one you want, need and love. I feel it!" He dropped to his knees. "Please marry me. I need you, Nora! I want you, I love you. I'm sorry! Please forgive me for not telling you sooner! I can't go through life without you!"

Nora grabbed her girls' hands, pulling them away from Stan. "Damn you! I can't stand a liar. Get away from me. Leave! I never want to see your face again! I hate you for lying to me!" She lost all resolve. She screamed, "I hate you! I hate you! I hate you! Leave now and never come back!" She turned and led her daughters away.

Martina was frantic. "No, Momma! I want Daddy!" She pulled her little hand free from Nora's grasp, leaping back into Stan's arms. "I love you, Daddy. Don't go! Please don't go, Daddy!"

Martina was crying uncontrollably. Cassandra was sobbing. Nora's own reaction wasn't far behind. She tightened the grasp on Cassandra's hand.

Stan held Martina and stood up to face Nora. He had tears in his eyes, silently whispering, begging her not to go. She walked up, grabbed her youngest daughter as Martina struggled against her, but she roughly pulled the screaming child away from him. Nora forcibly dragged her girls toward the door leading to the church basement. They cried as they struggled to break free, to run to Stan.

She glanced back at Stan one last time. He was on his knees, head in his hands. Tim and two brothers stood behind him, fists clenched. *And to think I loved you.*

***

Clara helped her daughter carry the sleeping girls to the Tahoe. Poor Nora was emotionally drained. The rehearsal for the marriage she didn't want had been dragging on when Stan had appeared. Her daughter's emotions went from surprise to elation when he said he wanted her to be his wife, then to anger when he said his divorce was final, and then to sadness as she'd pulled her girls away from him.

Clara's heart went out to her daughter. In the downstairs of the church, she encouraged Nora to be strong, warning her not to settle in life. Thank God Nora finally listened. When Tim walked in on them, Nora told him they were through. He ranted, raved and called her several very nasty names. He told her to go to Hell before slamming the door.

While Nora was strapping the girls in the back, Clara crawled into the passenger's side. There were things on the driver's seat that hadn't been there before.

"Nora, what's this? Who put these here?"

Nora pushed the driver's seat back, "What, Mom?"

"Well, it looks like a set of car keys."

Nora drew in a deep breath. She apparently recognized the keys and held them tightly to her chest.

"They're Stan's set of keys to the Tahoe and my apartment."

Clara opened up the plastic case. "A cassette tape? Muppet Show Cast Album?"

Nora looked away from her. "Stan must have left it for the girls. It's their favorite, Mom. He played it constantly for them."

"And what's this blue paper? It looks like a title to a car, uh, a Chevy Tahoe." She drew a deep intake of air. "On my God, Nora, it's for this vehicle. He signed the car over to you!"

"What?" screamed Nora as she pulled the paper from her mother's grip. Nora's hands trembled as she read it with her own eyes.

Clara examined the last thing, a piece of paper. *It can't be.* Nora was watching her. Clara's mouth was open wide, but she couldn't speak. With shaking hands, she handed the paper to Nora.

Nora read it and her face paled. Her hand went to her mouth and she sobbed.

"Nora, did I read that right? Tell me what it is."

"It's a receipt for Bob's hospital bill. Paid in full."

"Nora, what does all this mean?"

Tearfully, she responded, "It means Stan made my life much easier than it was. It means I can finally make a life for my little girls without the mountain of debt I was under. Oh God, why did he have to lie to me about his marriage?"

"But why would he give these things to you, Nora?"

She sadly turned to Clara. "He did it because he loves me."

Clara brushed the hair from her daughter's eyes. "You love him too, don't you?"

Nora stared out the window. "Yes, Mom. I love him very much. But he lied to me, can you understand that? I can't live with that. He lied to me! Why?"

Clara thought she understood. Her response was very quiet. "Maybe because when you love someone, you want them to be happy."

Nora slammed her hands against the steering wheel. "I was happy, when I was with him! He knew that and yet, he lied to me."

Clara was silent for a second before speaking. "Did you tell him you were happy when you were with him? I'm not sure you did. Instead, I think you lied to Stan, too."

Nora wiped her cheeks. "What do you mean?"

"You told him you were happy with Tim. He respected that. Maybe that was why he lied to you. Could it be that he tried to put your feelings first?"

"But that doesn't excuse it. He should have told me about his divorce."

Clara laughed. Nora turned to stare at her. Clara touched her arm.

"Yes, he should have. And no, it doesn't excuse his lie, but there is a Bible verse I want to remind you of."

"Great. A Bible lesson. What's that, Mom?"

"It goes something like, 'before you remove the speck from your neighbor's eye, take the log out of your own eye first'."

Nora shook her head. "Why are you siding with him?"

Clara grasped her hands. "Maybe Stan and I have something in common. Could it be he did what he did so you could be happy? Because he thought you were happy with what's his name? Despite his own feelings or desires."

Nora continued to shake her head.

Clara squeezed Nora's hands tightly. "I also want you to be happy, so a word of caution. Before you get your feathers in a ruffle over him lying to you, remember you also lied. Is there a big difference between what both of you did?"

Nora blubbered her response. "But don't you get that he lied to me about his marriage? Don't you comprehend that?"

Clara stared at her daughter strangely for a second. "When he interrupted the rehearsal, you knew it was his voice, didn't you?"

Nora was trying to wipe the tears from her eyes. "Of course I did."

"You were surprised... no, you *hoped* he would come. And when he did... when he spoke, your face lit up. You can't deny it. I saw your expression. Why would that be? How did he even know you were getting married? How did he know which church you were at?"

"Tim told him we were getting married on Saturday. I guess he checked around and found out where."

There's more to this story. "Nora, he said he lied to you because he had your best interests in mind. Why would he change his mind all of a sudden?"

"I don't know. Maybe because I sent him a goodbye letter."

"Oh, I see. And what did this letter say?"

"Mom, stop this! It's not making matters any better."

"Answer my question. What did you put in that letter?"

Nora hesitated. "I... I told him how much I loved him. I told him I shouldn't have let him leave on Christmas morning, and don't ask about what happened on Christmas morning. I told him I would have left Tim for him in a heartbeat. I told him I didn't care if he was married or not. I told him I would love him forever."

Her mother studied her face before continuing, "And what did you expect when he arrived? Did you suddenly think it would be like it was in high school when you almost left Bob for him?"

Nora's mouth dropped open. "I never told anyone about that! How did you know?"

"You'd married and moved away. But you left your diary. Once when I was cleaning, it fell to the floor. It opened to that page and I read it. I really wish you would have told me about it when it happened, but it was too late. You had already been married for a couple of years and were pregnant with Cassie."

"Mom, that was personal! You had no right!"

"No, I didn't, but that's water under the bridge. Now back to today, did you expect him to be single or married when he showed up tonight?"

"I thought he would be... well... that he would be... *married.*"

"So, it would have been okay if he was married? Now, he's single and so are you. I didn't read all of your diary, just the part about Stan. You know, I may be old and only your mother, but I could tell he was your true love, your eternal soulmate. Do you agree?"

A new set of tears erupted. It was almost five minutes before Nora could speak. "Yes, yes he is. Stan is my true love. But Mom, he..."

Clara put her finger to Nora's lips. "Shush. Sweetheart, I really want you to be happy and not have any regrets later. Put aside your pride and think about this. Both of you lied to each other, but that can be forgiven. The door to your happiness isn't yet closed. Your true love is still there. Put yourself in his shoes. Think how hard this must have been for him tonight. I don't believe he showed up for himself, but for you! For you and the girls. It's not too late. Do you see what I'm saying? You can still be happy, but the choice is now yours. If the door closes, you are the one who gave it that final push."

Nora looked at Clara and didn't say another word. She just stared at her mother.

***

His life didn't really matter anymore. He tried to push Nora out of his mind, but thoughts of her haunted his dreams and monopolized his days. *What's she doing now?* Was she on her honeymoon with Tim? Where were her two little girls? Did she leave them with Clara?

His head was spinning as he tried to put them out of his mind. But he couldn't. He'd lost Nora. Again. Only this time, it was final, forever. He was in his new house, but it would never be a home, not without Nora.

Starting Monday, Stan did the only thing he knew to do. He threw everything he had into his job. His personal life might be screwed up, but he still had his profession and by damn, he would excel at it.

By Friday evening, he was physically as well as mentally exhausted. Every muscle in his body was sore. He had a headache that would kill a cow. He could no longer focus. The clock in his office read a quarter of ten, long after everyone else had left for the weekend.

As he drove home, he listened to "Sweet Dreams," a sad and lonely Patsy Cline tune. When it was over, he would rewind and repeat the song. *Never dreamed a broken heart could hurt this badly.* His street came into view. Stan drove slowly because of his exhaustion.

Phantom visions of little animals running in front of him made him slow down even further.

Stan turned into his driveway, his headlights shining on... *No, can't be.* He buried his head in his hands. *My sanity's gone. I've finally lost my mind.*

Stan jumped when a knock sounded on the window. His mouth dropped open when he saw who it was. *Nora!*

Nora was standing outside his window. He quickly opened the door before her image vanished. Her face sported a smile as she warmly grabbed his hands. *Did I die and go to heaven?* She started to say something, but apparently changed her mind. She grabbed his neck and kissed him deeply, her taste making him forget about his exhaustion.

Stan wrapped his arms around her, afraid to let go. Afraid this vision would pass.

That wonderful voice whispered to him. "Oh, Stan..."

This is real. "Why are you here? You should be on your honeymoon. Is everything all right? Are the girls okay?"

She had the broadest smile he could recall. "Nothing's wrong and we're all fine. So why am I here? I hoped you knew. I couldn't marry Tim."

He looked quizzically at her, but before he could speak, she continued.

"How could I marry him? I didn't love him. Never did. I was only marrying him because I couldn't have you. I needed to look out for the girls. But, I got to thinking, how could I marry someone else when I was madly in love with you?" She kissed him again. "Sorry I came?"

Stan opened his mouth, but nothing came out. He could only shake his head no.

Nora laughed. The sound echoed joyously in Stan's ears. "I was wondering if we could go inside. The girls and I have been parked out here since four. We're freezing and I really have to pee! I was hoping and praying Gwen gave me the right address."

Stan stared in wonder. "Gwen gave you my address?"

"Yes, I tried to think of a way to find you. It finally struck me Wednesday that if anyone would know, she would. She came to see me yesterday with it on a slip of paper and told me that you weren't on a trip. Then she hugged me before wishing both of us good luck."

He kissed her again, then helped her carry the girls into the house. He was fighting back tears, but this time, they were tears of joy! The only bed with a mattress was his king bed. They deposited the girls there, covering them in rich fleece blankets. The girls were so tired that neither of them woke up. Hand in hand, Stan gave Nora the grand tour of the house starting with the bathroom.

She gazed in amazement at the size and beauty of the home. "Stan, this place is perfect. And it's yours?"

He gently took her hand and swung her around to see his face. "Half an hour ago it was just a house. Now it's a *real* home—because you are here. And no, it isn't mine... It's *ours*, if you'll share it with me. Marry me, please?"

Her smile was the most beautiful sight he'd ever seen. "Thought you'd never ask."

Chapter 16

Jeremy was keeping his in-laws company in the cardiac unit. The four sisters left him in the hospital room while they went to the cafeteria. Jeremy volunteered to stay, not out of duty, but out of love. He felt closer to Nora and Stan than he ever had with his own parents. At the family's request, Nora had been moved into the same room as Stan after surgery. Their beds were side by side. At Kaitlin's suggestion, their hands had been placed next to each other. Jeremy's eyes had been slowly rolling out of focus when a movement caught his attention. Jeremy shook his head, staring in disbelief. Stan was holding Nora's hand!

He quickly texted Kaitlin. Within five minutes, all four sisters were back in the room. Over the next half hour, they watched first Stan, then Nora start to move. Nora moaned, but everyone could see that the grip they had on each other grew tighter.

Nora was the first to wake up. Her daughters surrounded her. The first words from her lips were, "Is Daddy okay? Where is he?"

Martina placed her cheek against her mother's head. "Daddy's right next to you, Mom."

Nora looked intently at Stan for a moment before redirecting her gaze to her daughters. "Almost died, didn't I?"

Kelly answered in a broken voice, "It was touch and go for a while. I don't know how much you remember, but you fell and broke your hip. Then," Kelly's voice rose an octave, "you had a heart attack. Ninety percent blockage in two arteries. You coded, Mom, but they brought you back. They placed stents in your veins and the doctors are hopeful you'll make a full recovery."

"I thought so. I was outside my body, watching you. I saw them working on Daddy's body, saw you there kneeling next to me on the floor. Then Daddy was there, holding me tightly before telling me he was going back."

The four sisters stared at each other in disbelief. Kaitlin was the first to get her thoughts together. "Momma, for a while it looked like we would lose both of you." Her voice broke. "We c-couldn't... have..."

Nora patted her hand. "Don't you worry about that. We're both back and plan on staying here." Turning to Kelly, she said, "Okay, my favorite nurse, talk to me about the recovery plan." She pointed at Kaitlin's belly. "I've got grandbabies to spoil, you know?"

The conversation sapped Nora's energy, but she forced herself to remain awake. She was groggy when Stan regained consciousness about an hour later. Nora gently called his name.

A smile covered his face as he beamed at his wife. The first words out of Stan's mouth were, "You made it! I love you, sweetheart!"

"I love you too, Stan! I knew you'd come back. Couldn't make it through this life without you." Even though their family surrounded them, they didn't seem to notice. They talked to each other as if no one else existed.

***

Valentine's Day was their forty-first anniversary. Nora woke to see her husband smiling at her. They snuggled for a long time without making any attempt to get out of bed. Nora gazed lovingly into his eyes before gently pressing her lips to his.

Stan whispered into her ear, "It was forty-one years ago that we said 'I do'. Ever regretted it?"

Nora smiled at this man she loved, bringing his hand to her lips. "The only regret I have is that we didn't run away that first day I met you, in the school lobby. Remember?"

His eyes twinkled. "How could I forget? That was the first day I heard your voice—the voice of an angel."

She laughed as she ran her hand through his gray hair. "The girls all made fun of you because your zipper was down, but that isn't what I remembered most about you that day."

His laughter was the sound of joy in her ears. "Really? I thought that was what made you like me." Her cheeks warmed. "What do you remember about that first day?"

Her eyes smiled at the remembrance. "It was a combination of the jitters, excitement and affection. You know, you were all I could think about that night, and almost every night since." She brushed her fingers against his cheek.

He kissed those fingers. "Did I ever tell you that the first time I saw you, I told my friend Jeff I was going to marry you some day?"

She smiled slyly. "So, one look was all it took? You were done, giving your heart away to some girl you'd never seen before?"

The look Stan gave her swelled her heart. "When you see the one person God intended for you to be with, yes. And if we never got together, you'd still be the person I loved most in my life." His smile left. "Nora, in our life together, have I made you truly happy?"

Tears filled her eyes and she hugged her husband. She gently kissed him again. "Yes, yes! I never really knew happiness until I met you. I fell in love with you in high school and never fell out of love. I can tell you now, every day since we met, I thanked God for you. I asked Him to watch over you. When you came back into my life, I asked God to find some way to make you mine. I love you, so much more than words can ever explain."

They snuggled for a moment before she continued, "Now, it's your turn. Have I made you happy?"

"I don't have the words in me to tell you how I truly feel. Every single one of my dreams of romance, marriage and happiness were blown out of the water by you. *Happy* doesn't even begin to describe it. I love you, Nora!" He kissed his wife.

She didn't say anything for a while. Her emotions got in the way. "You realize there's a double-edged sword that comes with this type of intimacy. We dodged the bullet this time, but one of these days, one of us will leave the other behind. For the one who remains, life will be filled with loneliness. It will be un-bearable and un-thinkable. Whoever remains will never know happiness again."

Stan nodded as his eyes filled. "I agree, but maybe God will bless us by letting us go together. If He doesn't, we can comfort ourselves in the fact that the parting will be short. I truly believe that when we both pass on, we will be together for all of eternity. Do you remember when both of us were close to death?"

"Vividly."

"Remember how we connected?" Again, she nodded as she felt a smile grace her lips. He gently said, "I believe that was a brief glimpse into eternity. But if this is all there is, I can tell you with everything in my body and soul, I would not have passed up our love for anything. If we really are just like a wisp of smoke blown away by the winds of time, I am glad it was you. But we were... are... and *always will be* together. I love you, forever, Nora." He kissed his bride of forty-one years.

She kissed him back. "I love you, forever, Stan." They snuggled the morning away as they dreamed of eternity.

The End

Other Books by this Author

Seeking Forever (Book 1)

Kaitlin Jenkins is selected to embark on a six-month work project, out of her comfort zone and far away from her support network. If only she hadn't been assigned such a distractingly handsome partner—a former Army Ranger.

Jeremy is making his first foray into the civilian world. But he was not prepared to spend half a year on the road with a woman who seems even more heartless than his ex-wife.

Can love overcome the misunderstandings between them and the challenges of life on the road?

Seeking Happiness (Book 2)

Kelly lives a very happy life. A great marriage, four wonderful kids and a fulfilling job managing an emergency department in L.A. But the day after her sister's wedding, her husband breaks the news. He is leaving her for Hollywood's hottest young actress. Kelly's world crumbles around her.

Then she meets the man of her dreams – smart, cute and romantic. The love of her life. And that's when the trouble really begins. Will she fill the hole in her heart? Will she ever find happiness and love again?

Seeking Happiness is the second book in the Seeking Series, which revolves around the love and lives of the Jenkins family.

About the Author

Chas Williamson is a life-long Pennsylvanian. Over his life, he has been many things: husband, father, grandfather, amateur historian, as well as a story teller. The desire to write started at a very early age. For years, storytelling was only verbal, but in 2013, a work crisis was looming as his employer of 30-plus years decided to close. His wife encouraged him to use writing as an outlet to reduce stress. When he balked, she asked him to write a short love story. That story grew into what would later become *Seeking Forever*. It continued to blossom into three other books of the Seeking Series and then a second series. The characters he has created are very real to him, like real life friends and he hopes they become just as real to you.

Made in the USA
Columbia, SC
19 September 2018